MADE IN MIAMI

MADE IN MIAMI

by

Charles Willeford

POINTBLANK

Set in Sabon

POINT*BLANK* is an imprint of Wildside Press
www.pointblankpress.com
www.wildsidepress.com

Series Editor JT Lindroos
Copy edited by Robert D. Kelly

For more information contact Wildside Press

ISBN: 0-8095-7246-X / 978-0-8095-7246-5

ONE

THE Filipino houseboy was conscious now and began to bang his head up and down on the floor and kick some with his bound feet. His hands and feet were tightly wrapped with copper wire and there was a dishcloth gag in his mouth. Although he couldn't make much noise on the thickly-carpeted floor, his struggling annoyed Ralph at his work. Carefully placing the roll of red and yellow primacord on the end table by the fireplace, Ralph crossed the room to the Filipino and kicked the struggling little man in the head.

"Cut it out," Ralph sharply advised, "or I'll put you out altogether."

Despite the admonition the frightened houseboy banged his head on the carpeted floor again, terrified sienna eyes popping in his almost bloodless face. Ralph rolled the houseboy over on his stomach with a well-placed kick in the ribs, bent down and slugged the little man hard behind the ear with the pair of heavy pliers. The struggling stopped.

Ralph looked at his watch. Five-thirty. He had at least two more hours before Donald McKay and Tarzan would arrive. The wall safe wouldn't be too hard to blow—they were always built of thin plate metal. Good enough, maybe, to hold a wife's jewelry, but not strong enough to hold pornography. Blackmail pornography. And blackmail pornography was what Ralph Tone was after.

A large oil painting, secured to the wall by hinges, had covered the safe, and Ralph now closed it over the metal door. He made three tight loops of primacord around the frame. Then he carefully wired a detonating cap to the cord, attached double ends of copper wire to the cap, and played out the wire from the spool, backing slowly across the wide living room and into the kitchen. He set down the spool, went back for his battery blaster, retreated again to the kitchen, lifted the plunger and attached negative and positive wires. He made another trip through the luxuriously furnished living room and opened the first door leading off the hallway. There were eight similar doors, and each one of them opened into a bedroom. Searching through the first bedroom closet, Ralph found a quilt and an electric blanket on the shelf.

He returned to the living room and arranged the blanket and the quilt over the picture frame. As long as he had the time he might as well play it safe and muffle the explosion. Ralph opened the front door and made a brief reconnaissance. His car was well hidden, and couldn't be seen from the front porch. There was a broad sweep of lawn between the house and the road, and little danger of a passing car hearing any noise. The one house nearby had been unoccupied for two years, so that was safe, too.

To make certain no one was in the area Ralph circled the house for a look and reentered by the front door. He closed and bolted the door, entered the kitchen, swung the door to and pressed the plunger. Beneath the quilt and blanket there was a whooshing explosion. After raising the plunger Ralph returned to the living room. The door to the safe gaped open; the shattered picture frame had sailed clear across the room, a section of the plaster ceiling had dropped on the floor, and by a freak accident, a white ceramic-topped table had blown apart while its matching mate was unharmed. The houseboy had been blasted into consciousness again and his brown face powdered white by exploding plaster. His body trembled and his eyes were open, but he no longer struggled to get free.

Ralph began to pull graphic filth out of the safe. There were six reels of 16mm film in cans, and he tossed them into the fireplace. He next removed four stacks of eight-by-ten black and white photographs. The stacks of photos were divided into four general obscene classifications: pictures of men and women, of women and women, men and men, and pictures of men, women and animals.

Ralph began shuffling through them looking for the photos of Maria, but with a grunt of disgust he tossed the rest of the photos into the fireplace on top of the films. There were several hundred negatives, each in a four-by-five-inch brown slip over, still in the safe. He dumped the stacks of negatives into the fireplace. There wouldn't be time to examine all of the negatives to find the ones of Maria.

Ralph took the dynamite from its hiding place beneath a sparkleberry bush and brought it inside. After wiring six ten-inch sticks together he shoved them under the pile of films and photos in the fireplace. He would have preferred to burn the film, but didn't want smoke coming out of the chimney. With the temperature at ninety degrees in Dade County, Florida, a daytime fire would be noticed.

He turned his attention to the door. With strips of tape he covered the back of the door with sticks of dynamite, taped six more by the lock, and several extra sticks by the hinges. Now the ticklish part. He inserted the caps, one in the charge inside the fireplace and four more in the massed sticks on the back of the door.

The house was air-conditioned, but despite the evenly-distributed coolness, Ralph was perspiring freely. His dark blue T-shirt was almost black with perspiration, and big drops of sweat rolled down his nose and dropped on his hands as he measured the copper wire. He cut ten lengths, attached the loose ends to the five caps and, with his electric soldering iron, fixed the other packed wire ends to the left side of the electric buzzer beside the door.

Ralph collected his tools and dropped them into the toolbox. Before leaving the room he examined again the door buzzer and the wires leading to the caps in the dynamite. It would work, all right. There was no doubt in his mind. Altogether, there were forty-eight sticks of dynamite, and when the doorbell was pressed from the outside the door would blast outward, big chunks and splinters of hard maple would hurtle through the air, and whoever was standing on the porch...

What about the Filipino houseboy? He was one of them; he worked for McKay, and he should accompany him to hell. Ralph took the little man's feet and dragged him over closer to the door. He checked the copper wire around the houseboy's feet and around his arms behind his back. Tight.

Ralph picked up his toolbox, and stopped in the kitchen for a long pull of ice water from the jug in the refrigerator. Remembering how muggy the weather was outside, and how stifling it would be waiting in his car, he took the bottle of water with him when he left by the back door. He circled the house and struck out across the front lawn to the road, carrying the heavy toolbox in his left hand and the jug of water in his right.

He dashed across the unpaved, narrow road before the house, and entered the woods. He put the toolbox in the trunk of his car and then slid under the wheel. He could see across the road and the lawn without difficulty by looking through the trees, but he could not be spotted unless someone knew he was there. He waited, slapping at mosquitoes and wiping the perspiration from his face and neck with the tail of his T-shirt.

His watch now said six-thirty, but the sun was still bright in the cloudless sky, and sundown wasn't until seven-fifteen. After sundown, there would still be an afterglow of dusk for fifteen or twenty minutes, but before it got completely dark, Mr. McKay and his bodyguard, Tarzan, would wheel up in front of the house to prepare for the big Saturday night orgy. McKay would tell Tarzan to ring the bell for the houseboy to open the door, and then...

I'll sit here and watch the explosion, Ralph thought, but I won't think about it. I would rather think about Maria, and the way she was then. Not the way she is now—the way she was then...

TWO

THE comedian was working very hard.

"When I got out of my cab in front of my hotel, the doorman grabbed the suitcase out of my hand. I reached into my pocket to give him a tip but I didn't have any change. 'I'm sorry,' I said, 'but I don't have any change with me.' So the doorman says, 'How much have you got?' Well I looked in my wallet then. And I said, 'I've got a dollar.' Well, the doorman gave me this look, raring back, don't you know, like a nervous stud inspecting a Shetland pony mare, and he says, 'My good man, my young tourist friend, in Miami Beach a dollar *is* change!'"

And the expected laughter rose from the crowd in the Rotunda Room.

Ralph Tone, standing beside his elevator in his skintight red and blue uniform, sighed deeply. The voice of the comedian carried into the lobby over the P.A. system from the Rotunda Room loud and clear, and Ralph had been listening to the comedian's routines (all three of them) for more than a month, running the elevator up and down in between on the eight P.M. to six A.M. shift. The Rotunda Room of the Rotunda Hotel had a floor show at ten, twelve, and at three in the morning. Several regular guests, all oldsters, sat in the lobby reading the paper or watching television in the sunken section beyond the desk. They paid no attention to the speakers crackling from the ceiling. The comedian now turned to song, an imitation of Jerry Lewis imitating Al Jolson singing "Mammy," backed up by the Rotunda Trio; guitar, piano and drums.

Sighing again, Ralph wished a passenger would appear so he could whisk him upstairs and get away from the comedian's voice. Not that Skippy didn't try hard, because he did, but he was cheap entertainment, just barely good enough for the summer crowd at the Rotunda Hotel. Most of the guests at the Rotunda were easterners from New Jersey and New York, down for a week or ten days on a package vacation with an airline or railroad. In addition to their passage to and from New York, their hotel room was thrown in (Seven dollars a day, Minimum, Double Occupancy,

European Plan) and the Rotunda had to keep expenses down to break even.

During the winter season, from November 15 through April 15, the same room renting for seven dollars a day, per person double occupancy, would leap to fifteen dollars a day. Then the Rotunda Room would be renovated, linen tablecloths instead of cotton prints would appear on the tables, drinks would climb from $.65 to $1.10, and there would be name entertainers and name bands in the Rotunda Room.

For the thousandth time in thirty days Ralph cursed the decision that had brought him to Miami Beach with his buddy, Tommy Grant, instead of to Asheville, North Carolina. Many of his classmates at Florida State University had begged him to go to Asheville and work in the hotels there for the summer. "Maybe you don't make as much dough, Ralph, but at least it's cool, and you can have a hell of a good time."

But Tommy had convinced him otherwise. "Look, Ralph," he had said earnestly, "Miami Beach isn't like it used to be. All of the hotels are staying open in summer now instead of closing, and we should be able to make twice as much money as these guys going to Carolina. Sure, it'll be hot, but that's to our advantage. We won't have as much competition when we look for jobs."

Tommy had been wrong both ways. Not only was the competition stiff, they weren't making as much money in Miami Beach as they would have made in Asheville. Ralph had landed a job, finally, running an elevator on the night shift, and Tommy had wound up as a busboy, both of them at the Rotunda Hotel. Although Tommy Grant had now advanced to the exalted status of Head Busboy, where he got a small percentage of the waiter's tips, Ralph was still stuck with the night shift on the elevator. If he could only get on the day shift, he might be able to take on another job at night somewhere, either as a busboy, or maybe as counterman at one of the strip eateries. But after being up all night, standing on his feet, he was dead tired when morning came around, and didn't feel up to looking for a daytime job.

By living like a monk, Ralph had saved more than a hundred dollars, but he certainly wasn't going to have enough money saved by the end of summer to get through the fall semester without working again. He would have to take his job as waiter again at the Co-op, in addition to his all-day Saturday job at the gas station. The G.I. Bill helped, but it didn't help enough, not for an art student anyway. After paying his tuition and laying in art materials and books for the semester, there was precious little money left out of this $120.00 a month from the Korean G.I. Bill.

The only real break Ralph had had at the Rotunda Hotel was when he had met Mr. Donald McKay. Mr. McKay was one of the owners of the hotel—there was a corporation of some kind, and Mr. McKay had some capacity on it, Ralph didn't know what— and he had one of the $100-a-day penthouse suites all year round. In addition to the suite he owned a thirty-foot cabin cruiser and a home in the country. He seemed to have more money than he knew what to do with, and he had taken a liking to Ralph. Twice now, Ralph had gone fishing with Mr. McKay and was going again the next day, and he looked forward to being out on the water all afternoon.

The last time Mr. McKay had taken him fishing they had pulled into the Marina about three in the afternoon, and Mr. McKay had asked Ralph to go shopping with him on Lincoln Road. Tarzan, Mr. McKay's bodyguard, (boat crew, and chauffeur for the Caddy) had driven them from the Marina to Lincoln Road, and then followed along in the street, double-parking as Ralph and Mr. McKay shopped in various exclusive stores.

All Ralph had said was, "I like that on you," or "That doesn't suit you, Mr. McKay," all afternoon, and the rich man had bought him a fifty-dollar sport coat. After Tarzan dropped him off at his rooming house, Ralph had taken his own car and driven back to the exclusive shop, returned the sport coat and picked up the fifty dollars in cash. The proprietor, a small bald man in black Italian silk, had presented Ralph with two five-dollar sport shirts for merely bringing Mr. McKay into the store.

"I've got to think of a way to make some more money," Ralph thought again for the thousandth time, and then he stopped thinking altogether and just stared, with his mouth partly open.

Coming toward the elevator from the Rotunda Room was Miss Maria Dugan, and for a change she didn't have her roommate, Miss Peggy Vittorni, with her. Maria Dugan was one of the guests, and in Ralph's opinion, the most beautiful girl in the hotel. That was saying a great deal, because the ratio of guests at the Rotunda ran close to twelve women for every man.

Maria was tall and gorgeous, with thick, lustrous dark hair, as black as midnight. She wore her hair short, and ordinarily Ralph didn't go for women with cropped locks. But Maria's hair was so inky black, and framed her ivory oval face so perfectly, Ralph couldn't picture her wearing it any other way. There was just enough natural curl to give her face a gamin look. The contrast between her black hair and pale skin was almost breathtaking. Maria's features were even, her nose was straight, and although her mouth was a trifle large, her teeth were white and small, endowing her with a beautiful smile. She was wearing a white silk cocktail gown as she rustled across the lobby, and although her beauty had been wasted on the group of female guests in the Rotunda Room, it wasn't wasted on Ralph. He watched her daintily-rounded figure as she entered the elevator, and carefully averted his eyes from the low-cut gown which exposed the cleavage of her hard, full breasts.

"Going up already, Miss Dugan?" Ralph asked politely. "The show isn't over, is it?"

"You mean the poor man's Milton Berle? Skippy McCarthy? No, he's still going on. And on and on and on," she added, her cinnamon-brown eyes glowing with merriment.

"He tries hard," Ralph said, laughing politely.

"He certainly does," Maria agreed. "I'm surprised he hasn't been signed up by television. Oh, his stolen jokes are all right, I suppose, but when he starts to sing—uh uh!" She tossed her curls and shook her head.

It's nice to be alone with her like this, Ralph thought, and to talk with her. As a rule Maria was always accompanied by her girl friend, who was as plain as a mud fence. It was always that way. Every good-looking girl always had an ugly one for a close friend and companion. Ralph had been stuck enough times on double dates to be familiar with the phenomenon, although he didn't know the reason for the rule.

"Say," Maria exclaimed. "This is the sixth floor already, and I get off on Four!" But she smiled.

"I'm sorry," Ralph said, flustered. He stopped the elevator, and started down. Maria's female scent was overpowering, a combination of perfume and musk. He stopped at the fourth floor, and opened the door. Maria stepped out, stopped momentarily to smooth the silk down over her gently swelling hips, and Ralph reached out impulsively and gripped her arm.

"Miss Dugan," he blurted, his face flushing with swift heat, "how would you like to go out on a boat with me tomorrow?"

Maria hesitated, and a narrow line formed between her arched brows. She glanced surreptitiously at Ralph's name tag, pinned on his blue-jacketed chest. "I don't know, Ralph," she said seriously. "My girl friend and I were to go to the Seaquarium tomorrow on the tour."

"You can go to the Seaquarium any time," Ralph pleaded. "And on the boat you might even catch some fish."

"Is it your boat, Ralph?"

"No. It belongs to a rich friend of mine."

"All right." Maria smiled. "What time tomorrow?"

"Nine o'clock. And I'd better meet you at the coffee shop on the corner. I'd pick you up here, but they've got some crazy rule about employees not dating the guests." Ralph flashed what he hoped was a winning smile. It was.

"Nine o'clock, then. That isn't a decent hour for a girl to get up on vacation, but I think I can make it."

"Wonderful! Good night, Miss Dugan."

"Good night, Ralph. And by the way, my name is Maria."

"Sure, sure. Good night, Maria."

The buzzer was going like crazy, and Ralph dropped down to the lobby. The floor show was over, and there was a rush for a while. Then the elevator business would be quiet until midnight except for the old people who went up and down all of the time. The old women especially; they were always forgetting something they had left in their room.

For the first time since coming to Miami Beach, Ralph was happy, and he was going to smile at all of the corny jokes for the rest of the night if it killed him. The most familiar gag was when a guest would say, "Your life sure has its ups and downs, doesn't it?" It was hard for Ralph to laugh at this hoary chestnut, but tonight he would try.

The only worry Ralph had was that he hadn't asked Mr. McKay if it would be all right to bring a girl along, but he didn't suppose the rich sportsman would mind. Not a pretty girl like Maria. When

Mr. McKay had bought him the sport coat he had thought that perhaps the man might be queer or something, but Mr. McKay hadn't made any passes at him yet. And several times Ralph had taken girls, really good-looking dolls, up to Mr. McKay's penthouse. So he supposed that McKay was just a good guy, even if he did have money, and wouldn't mind having Maria along. And if worse came to worst, he could take Maria for a boat ride on one of the charter boats. Ralph hadn't had a date since he came to Miami and he was sick of living like a hermit or something.

And that Maria was really beautiful, a real doll, a real live doll...

THREE

MARIA DUGAN closed the door behind her and tossed her room key and beaded bag on top of the disordered dresser. With two girls sharing the same quarters for four days, the room was pretty messy. In addition to the two sets of cosmetics on top of the dresser in plaid train cases, there were large boxes of Kleenex, sunburn lotion, spilled powder, combs, hairbrushes, and an over-flowing ashtray.

Both chairs in the room were piled high with clothing belonging to Maria and Peggy, and two still-wet bathing suits occupied the center of the blotter on the small writing desk beneath the window. Although 419 was listed as a double room by the Rotunda Hotel, the only reason it passed for a double was the pair of twin beds. The room was very small, but it had wall-to-wall carpeting, and the furniture was fairly modern. And, of course, it had a bathroom. No tub, just a shower, and the shower curtain wasn't long enough to keep the water off the bathroom floor. Whoever took the first shower had a definite advantage, but this was usually Maria, so Peggy was the one who was always complaining about the wet tile floor.

Maria unzipped her dress at the back and carefully slipped it over her head. She draped it lovingly over the foot of her bed while she looked for a coat hanger in the closet. It was the only really decent dress Maria had brought with her and she took ex-cellent care of it. The silk dress was much too good to wear in a Rotunda Room full of women while she drank Tom Collinses at sixty-five cents apiece, the waiter expecting a dime tip every time he brought another round. The Tom Collinses had tasted like lemonade anyway, and Maria thought she could drink a hundred of them and never feel anything. All of those women down there, craning their skinny necks every time a man came in, and when a man did come in he always had a girl with him. The floor show was lousy, and nobody had ever asked her for a dance, or paid for any of her drinks.

So far this vacation had been a bust for Maria, without a single date; but now, things were getting better. She had a date, even if he was only an elevator boy. At least Ralph was handsome, with his brown crinkly hair and shy brown eyes. It was kind of cute the way he had asked her for a date, and the only reason she had hesitated at all was because she didn't want to appear too anxious.

When she got back to New York she could embroider the story considerably for the girls in the office; tell them she went out on a rich man's yacht, and let them envy her. At least, going out on a boat would be more fun than following a group of girls around the Seaquarium looking at fish. She hadn't come to Miami Beach to look at a bunch of dumb fish. If she had wanted to see fish she could have stayed at home and looked at fish in the Fulton Market.

At first, travelling to Miami Beach had been a lot of fun, but the anticipation of the vacation during the last six months had been more fun than the actual experience. Maria and Peggy had planned their vacation carefully, putting five dollars apiece away every week and watching the savings grow in separate bank books, but the four days they had spent at the Rotunda so far had been as dull as dust.

She had paraded around the pool in her bathing suit, but except for the lifeguard, a whining old man in an old-fashioned gray bathing suit who was always blowing his silly whistle and telling everyone not to run on the wet pavement, there had been no one to admire her beauty except other women.

Pouting prettily, Maria stripped off her slip, undid her brassiere, and admired herself in the full-length mirror on the back of the bathroom door.

Maria pushed her panties down, stepped out of them, and walked closer to the mirror, the nap of rug prickling her bare feet. She faced the mirror, put her hands on her hips; and arms akimbo, turned first to the left, then to the right, her eyes admiring her mature figure, the full womanly hips, and long straight legs.

"You sure are beautiful," she whispered. And then she giggled girlishly.

From her Spanish mother Maria had inherited her black hair and dark brown eyes, but it was from her Irish father, Rodney Dugan, a barge captain on the Hudson for twenty-five years before his death, she had inherited her fair, white skin, and a sometimes violent temper. Maria stepped in close to the full-length mirror reflection, pressed her body against it, and kissed her bright red mouth against itself.

"I love you," she said. She really meant it.

There was a sound of a key in the door, and with a frightened cry, Maria opened the bathroom door and fled inside. But it was only Peggy Vittorni, her roommate, and next-desk neighbor at the Faultless Topcoat Company.

Ralph Tone hadn't been exactly fair in his appraisal of Peggy Vittorni. In her own way, Peggy was an attractive girl, but she was not as interesting in her face and figure as Maria. She was small and dark and Maria was tall and dark, but Peggy's shoulders slumped carelessly, which made her seem smaller and dumpier than she actually was. Her hips were wide and deep, and she had a small waistline and small breasts. Perhaps it was her preference in clothes that made her look short and dumpy; full-circle skirts and high-necked blouses. Men were always surprised, however, when they saw Peggy in a bathing suit stretched out on her back beside a swimming pool, because her figure was surprisingly good. Her complexion was poor, and she wore her black hair in bangs over her forehead to hide a scattering of pimples. With a pair of heavy tortoise-shell glasses on her nose, Peggy always seemed to have an owlish look and didn't appear quite bright.

But of the two, Peggy was the steadier, and she was cunning when it came to handling money. She was quite competent when arguing with salesgirls and travel agencies, and getting the most value out of every dollar. As Peggy entered the room she was smiling, and called out gaily to Maria in the bathroom:

"You really should have stayed, Maria. You missed the best part!"

Maria kicked the bathroom door open. "You don't have to shout at me. I can hear you. And as far as I'm concerned I didn't miss a thing."

"Oh, but you did," Peggy laughed, remembering.

"I doubt it." Maria had slipped a shorty nightgown over her head and was busily slapping blobs of cold cream on her face and neck. "I think that Skippy character is corny."

"Sure he is!" Peggy laughed. "That's why he's so funny. I think he's good myself. You miss the whole point sometimes, Maria. You've got to get the spirit of things if you want to have any fun."

"I'm entering into the spirit tomorrow." Maria said. "I'm going out on a rich man's yacht."

"Honest?"

"That's right. While you and all those school teachers are trooping around the Seaquarium, I'm going to be out on the ocean drinking champagne, and basking in the sun."

"I don't believe it. Where did you meet a rich man with a yacht?"

"Right here in the hotel." Maria smiled enigmatically.

"What's his name?"

"Don't you wish you knew?" Maria teased.

"I think you're mean, Maria. We don't have to go to the Seaquarium if you don't want to, but I've got the tickets for the tour and everything."

"No, it isn't exactly a rich man," Maria smiled at her friend. "But I do have a date for a change. And I'd rather have a date to go out on a boat than visit the Seaquarium. You can get the money back on my ticket."

"Don't worry," Peggy said grimly. "I'll get the money back all right! Who asked you for a date?"

"One of the fellows who works here at the hotel."

"Which one?"

"What difference does it make? I hardly know him, but if he has a friend, maybe I can get us a double date to go out one night before we leave. Do you realize that we have less than three more days to go before we have to go back, and this is the first date I've had?"

"I'm having fun, Maria, seeing everything and all. I don't care whether I have a date or not."

"Well, I do! I'm tired of paying for my own drinks and dinner. I thought there would be all kinds of men down here—you remember what the woman at the travel agency said? Wait until I see her—I'm going to tell her a few things!"

Peggy laughed. "No, you won't. I know you too well, Maria. You'd never admit to anybody that you went four days in Miami Beach without being asked for a date."

Maria smiled ruefully. "I suppose you're right. Anyway, I've got a date tomorrow."

"I hope you have a good time."

"I hope so, too." Maria turned to her friend, dabbed at her heavily creamed face with a wad of tissue.

"Honestly, Peggy, I haven't had any fun since we got here. It isn't at all what I expected. It's been so hot and all, and much more expensive than we planned."

"Our budget is doing okay."

"I know. But except for the hotel, I don't feel like going to a night club by myself—I mean, two girls going into bars all alone—it isn't right. You feel like you're trying to pick somebody up or something. I'm sorry I came. It would have been more fun to stay home and have Sidney take me out. I could have slept late in the mornings and gone to movies in the afternoon. Did I tell you that Sidney asked me to marry him?"

Peggy's eyes widened, and she took off her glasses. "You sure know how to keep a secret!" Peggy said resentfully. "You never told me anything about it before."

"I turned him down, that's why." Maria shrugged. "But I did it in such a way that he still has hope. I don't want to get married yet, but I don't want to lose my boy friend either." She giggled. "I don't want to work all my life typing in a room with thirty-nine other girls, but I'm not ready to get married yet, and certainly not to Sidney."

"Do you love him?" Peggy asked hesitantly.

"I don't know what love is," Maria replied seriously. "If love is half as bad as all the popular songs make it out to be I hope I never fall in love. I don't know what I want, Peggy. I want something though, and something I've never had. There must be more to life than working eight hours a day, five days a week, nursing pennies, and riding the subway, and skimping all year long for one week in Miami Beach. And it hasn't been much fun either."

Maria went to the window and opened it as wide as it would go. She leaned out the window, frowning as she surveyed the view. Their fourth floor room was on the northern side of the hotel, and they couldn't see the ocean from the window. All Maria could see was the deep block-large hole in the ground and a short section of the highway. Contractors were excavating on the site next door to the Rotunda, and the sound of blasting and steam shovels woke the girls up every morning at seven-thirty A.M. Another new hotel would be erected on the site within a year, and a hotel less than twenty years old had been torn down to make room for the newer and larger structure.

"Have you admired our wonderful view lately?" Maria said sarcastically.

"I wouldn't stand at the window in my nightgown, Maria," Peggy said prudishly. "Not in that short gown, anyway. People looking in can see everything you've got."

"Nobody can see in on this side." Maria moved away from the window, however, and stretched out on her bed. Peggy flipped off the switch by the door and silently undressed by the light coming into the room from the open bathroom door. She creamed her face, and put on pajamas. There was a gentle breeze coming in from the window, and although the room was warm, the heat wasn't unbearable. An air-conditioned room would have added two dollars a day to the daily rate, and both girls had agreed to do without it.

Peggy sat down on the edge of Maria's bed and put her stubby hand on Maria's knee. Maria moved her legs open slightly and looked blankly at the ceiling.

"Have you ever let Sidney make love to you?" Peggy asked huskily.

"I've let him kiss me, if that's what you mean."

"No, that isn't what I mean, and you know it."

"I know what you mean, and the answer is no. Capital N, O! When a girl works for fifty dollars a week, she only has one thing to give her husband and that's her virginity. And believe me, the only way Sidney'll ever get it from me is with a ring on my finger!" she added grimly.

Peggy giggled. "Move over, you bum, and let me lie down!" Reluctantly, Maria squirmed over slightly, and Peggy stretched out beside her, sharing the pillow.

"You've got your own bed, you know," Maria reminded her friend.

"Remember how you and I used to practice kissing, Maria? Tongue kissing, and all?"

"All girls go through that phase, I suppose. Sure, I remember."

"Does Sidney ever kiss you like that?"

"Sometimes. Why?"

"I just wondered." Peggy was on her left side, and she ran her fingers lightly inside Maria's thigh. "Do you remember some of the other things we did, Maria, after school at my house, that summer when Mother was working at Mamie's Hat Shop?"

"Cut it out." Maria crossed her legs. "Of course I remember. But that was kid stuff, Peggy."

"It was fun though, wasn't it?"

"I suppose so. At the time, it was."

"How would you like to—?"

"Why don't you go to bed?" Maria said crossly. "I've got to get up early. Call down to the desk for me, Peg, and leave a call for seven-thirty. My date is for nine."

"All right." Peggy sighed, lifted the telephone and made the call. After replacing the receiver, Peggy went into the bathroom, removed her pajamas and took a long shower. She brushed her teeth, put her pajamas on again, and switched out the bathroom light.

"Maria," she whispered softly, leaning over the sleeping girl. "Are you awake?"

Maria didn't reply. Peggy got into her own bed, kicking the sheet angrily to the floor. She lay upon her back for more than an hour, arms at her sides, fists tightly clenched, staring at the ceiling with her 70 – 30 eyes (correctible to 30 – 20 with glasses) before she could fall asleep.

But Maria slept soundlessly, sighing gently from time to time with pleasure, deep in wonderful dreams. She dreamed of handsome men in shiny armor, mounted on white horses, carrying bouquets cleverly fashioned out of money. And she dreamed of more handsome men in evening clothes, carrying roses and enormous sacks of money in canvas bags, and of white, shimmering castles, and of wine-dark yachts, riding at anchor on a viridian sea of shifting, floating, undulating—what was it?—money, money, money!

FOUR

SIX A.M. at the Rotunda Hotel, and Ralph Tone's eight-to-six long and boring shift on the elevator was over. He dropped from the lobby to the basement and shouted down the reverberating concrete hall to the locker room for his relief. A moment later, Johnny Townsend, a conscientious kid of seventeen who had run away from his home in Flint, Michigan, and who was passing himself off as a young man of twenty, came down the corridor buttoning his jacket.

"Don't get excited, Ralph, boy," Johnny said happily. "I've never failed you yet, have I?"

Ralph stepped into the hall and repeated his standing joke to his relief man, a gag that always made Johnny Townsend laugh, no matter how many times he heard it. He was really a good-natured boy, happy with his boring job, and ecstatic about his escape from Michigan and his father, who had threatened to send him to college.

"You'll find some people waiting on the main floor," Ralph said with a straight, serious face. "They're nice folks, so take them anywhere they want to go."

Johnny laughed. "Sure will, Ralph, sure will!" He laughed again, clanged the door shut, and shot up out of the basement.

Ralph stripped off his tight uniform, pulled on a pair of khaki twill shorts, and was dressed for the outside world. The white T-shirt he had worn beneath the blue uniform jacket was his upper outside garment, and he was already wearing socks and shoes. He hung his uniform neatly in his locker, closed the door and whirled the combination lock twice. He left by the basement exit and went into the parking lot reserved for employees on the north side of the hotel.

The sun was already up and Ralph could feel its tropical heat as he climbed into his car. By ten o'clock the land mass would be warmed by the sun—two more hours sooner than the ocean—the cool air from the sea would rush in to take the place of the hot air rising from the land and there would be a steady breeze on the beach for the rest of the day. But at six A.M. the humid air was still, and perspiration was flowing freely from Ralph's face and neck before he had his car started and turned on the highway.

Thinking pleasant thoughts about his date with Maria, Ralph tooled along the almost deserted road, relishing the openness of his car, his freedom from the claustrophobia of the elevator. This was the time of day he enjoyed most. The highway wasn't crowded, and he could cruise along and study the various designs of the motels along the beach. Some of them were really crazy: there were motels in the shape of castles, of pyramids, ships, Moorish harems, French chateaus, pre-historic animals, and God-knows-what-all. Side by side, each with its own narrow strip of private beach, with gleaming exotic neon signs, great expanses of colored glass, every motel along the strip vied with its neighbor to disguise its basic purpose: a lodging for the night. Someday, Ralph thought, when I become a famous artist, I'm going to come down here and design a motel that *looks* like a motel. He laughed to himself: What a radical idea!

At the 41st Street Bridge (Arthur Godfrey Road) Ralph turned inland and within a few minutes was parked at the curb in front of Mrs. Hirsch's Rooming House.

Now for a wonderful "natural diet" breakfast, Ralph thought bitterly as he climbed the porch steps and entered the musty hallway.

Mrs. Hirsch was a kind and generous woman. She fussed over her "boys" and thought of her roomers as her own sons. Her rates were cheap—forty dollars a month for room and board—and she provided clean sheets every Saturday and clean towels anytime they were needed. But the table she set three times a day caused a steady turnover of boarders. Because of the "natural diet" there had been boarders who had checked in and out again after only one meal.

Mrs. Hirsch was the president of the Miami Natural Diet Society and she practiced what she preached. Ralph had worked a ten-hour shift and had eaten a ham sandwich and a bowl of raspberry jello at midnight in the kitchen at the Rotunda Hotel, but he was now ravenously hungry again. To appease his hunger he would be forced to eat a meal of carrot juice, shredded lettuce, boiled radishes and celery *au natural jus*. He could top off this fine natural breakfast with more carrot juice, or if he wanted a hot drink, he could pour a cupful of boiling beet juice.

As the sullen boarders glumly picked at their breakfast, Mrs. Hirsch, from her place at the head of the table, queried them individually concerning bowel movements and the size and consistency of their stools. The tiny birdlike woman, with blue-gray hair piled high upon her head, chirped cheerfully and tirelessly, sipping daintily from a six-ounce glassful of carrot juice which, except for a few pieces of parsley at noon, was all she would have until she sat down to her main meal in the evening and ate a few leaves of boiled cabbage which would provide her with the necessary "roughage" for proper bowel movement.

It was worse if you complained. Mrs. Hirsch would cheerfully agree with you that the food was no good, but then food of any kind was no good! It was much better for your mind and body if you went on a fast, eating nothing whatsoever.

"Look at Gandhi!" she would cry ecstatically. "He fasted all the time, and the doctors who examined his body after his death said he had the corpse of a man only forty-five years old!"

Mrs. Hirsch frequently fasted for as long as ten days at a time, staggering weakly from room to room, sitting stiffly at mealtimes at the head of the table with only a glass of lukewarm water before her. At these times, when Mrs. Hirsch was slowly starving, her pale blue eyes sunk deep in their sockets, the boarders felt guilty when they ate a second helping of lettuce or drank an extra glassful of celery juice.

Following his breakfast, with hot beet juice and cold carrot juice blending resentfully in his stomach, Ralph climbed the stairs to the second story bedroom he shared with Tommy Grant. He was desperate for sleep, but afraid to lie down even for an hour. Staying awake was not a great problem, however. He had started taking benzedrine and dexedrine at college, and he popped two pink, heart-shaped dexedrine tablets into his mouth and entered the shower at the end of the upstairs hall. After a long rejuvenating shower and a slow, meticulous shave, Ralph returned to his room.

Tommy Grant appeared in the doorway just in time to catch Ralph in the act of stealing his blue Izod sport shirt out of the bureau drawer.

"Come on, Ralph," Tommy said angrily. "You're not going to

wear that; it's my best shirt!"

"I'll pay for the laundry," Ralph said, unbuttoning the shirt and tossing the cardboard backing on the floor. "I've got a date and I'm taking her out on Mr. McKay's boat."

"You would have a date. I'm off this morning and I thought we could go over to the beach and maybe pick up something."

"I've already picked up something. You know that really good-looking girl who always has that weird one following her around? Well, I got a date with her. Maria Dugan."

"You aren't supposed to date the guests, Ralph." Tommy reminded him.

"Yeah," Ralph replied. "Maybe I can get you a date with the friend and we can—"

"Don't do me any favors." Tommy Grant flopped across the unmade bed and lit a cigarette. He was a thin energetic boy from Georgia, and pronounced "favors" as "fay-eh-vohs."

Ralph draped a yellow silk scarf around his neck and stuffed the ends under the open collar of the blue sport shirt. Although a scarf was unnecessary in the blistering heat, he felt an open ascot added a note of sophistication to his appearance. He thrust his hairy legs into a pair of lemon-yellow Bermuda shorts, and then transferred keys, change and wallet into the pockets.

"If you don't look like a tourist I ain't never seen one," Tommy chuckled. "She ain't going to know you in that get-up."

Ralph grinned and pulled on a pair of black, knee-length socks. He slipped his long narrow feet into cordovan loafers, and brushed his curly brown hair at the mirror above the battered dresser.

"That's all right, boy," he said. "Those New York girls expect Floridians to dress this way. Seriously, how do I look?"

"You look fine, Ralph." Tommy got to his feet. "You can drop me off downtown, if you don't mind. I got to get me something to eat. My stomach thinks my throat is cut."

Ralph drove Tommy to a restaurant, and headed toward the vicinity of the hotel to meet his date.

Maria Dugan was already seated on a stool at the counter when Ralph entered the coffee shop at a quarter to nine. He dropped down beside her and asked the waitress for coffee by pointing to the urn and nodding.

"Hi, Maria," he said casually.

"Hello, there," she replied with a welcoming smile. "For a second I hardly knew you. You certainly look nice."

"Thank you. You look good enough to eat. Literally."

Maria laughed, and sipped her coffee. Her short black hair was tied with a broad red ribbon that matched her lipstick exactly. She wore a man's white shirt, with the sleeves rolled up, and the front was unbuttoned halfway down her chest, exposing the cleavage of her melon-heavy breasts. The shirt tails had been tightly tied about her narrow waist, emphasizing her slimness. A tight pair of red, cuffed shorts and a pair of sandals completed her costume.

As the waitress set his coffee down before him, Ralph's hairy knee touched the smoothness of Maria's bare leg and before he knew what he was doing he had put three spoons of sugar in his coffee.

"As long as I was going to meet you here, anyway," Maria said, to make conversation, "I thought I'd come over earlier and eat breakfast."

"Is that all you're having?" Ralph asked, pointing his chin at the glass of orange juice and cup of coffee in front of Maria.

"If a girl doesn't watch her weight, you know," Maria explained, "she'll get fat."

"Not you," Ralph said sincerely. "You've got the best figure I've ever seen. I mean it!"

Maria's ivory skin turned a shade of delicate rose. "Well, I'd like to keep it. And the only way I know is to watch my diet."

"You ought to live where I live then," Ralph laughed. He told Maria about the natural diet of Mrs. Hirsch's Boarding House, about her fasts, and queries into her boarders' bowel movements at the table. Within a few minutes they were laughing together as though they had known each other for years instead of minutes.

Ralph paid the checks, and took Maria on a guided tour of the Gold Coast, pointing out things she had missed on the Gray Line Tour, and showing her some of his favorite buildings. The young couple got along well together, both of them brimming with conversation which bubbled out of their lips in a constant stream, first one interrupting the other, laughter, and then the other breaking in again.

The morning passed swiftly and, until Maria reminded him, Ralph had completely forgotten about his promise to take her for a boat ride. He was supposed to meet Mr. McKay at the Marina at eleven-thirty, and he had to hustle through the swarming traffic to make it on time. After parking his car, Ralph took Maria's arm and marched her to the pier. He was still apprehensive about bringing an uninvited guest along, but his nervousness disappeared when he saw the delighted expression on Mr. McKay's face.

Donald McKay was a man in his early fifties who had lived well for most of his adult life, and he had the contented look of a pampered and well-fed cat. There was a sleekness about his appearance, from his smooth gray hair to his small, well-kept hands and feet. He had an affable manner, a cultured "Southern" voice, and a practiced habit of gallantry. He was, as usual, impeccably dressed.

Ralph introduced Maria to McKay. After welcoming her aboard, and seating her in a canvas captain's chair on the after-well deck, McKay congratulated Ralph on his excellent taste in women. McKay called to Tarzan to cast off, and asked Maria where she would like to go.

"Gee, I don't know, sir," Maria replied, embarrassed by the solicitous attention and the opulent appearance of the cabin cruiser.

McKay cast his head back and laughed softly with genuine but restrained amusement. "Sir!" he said, shaking his small head from side to side. "It's been a long time since a pretty girl called me 'sir'!"

"I—I—mean, Mr. McKay," Maria stammered, flushing to the roots of her dark hair.

"Call me Donald," Mr. McKay told her sincerely. "We don't have any formalities aboard the *Sea Witch*, but if you like you can call me Captain."

"All right," Maria smiled. "I like that. I think I'll call you Captain."

"Fine." McKay turned pleasantly to Ralph. "Why don't you take the wheel, Ralph, so I can introduce Maria to my crew?"

"Yes, sir," Ralph replied, and relieved Tarzan at the wheel. Ralph was pleased by the reception he and Maria had received. Steering the craft through the bay, dodging other boats, slowing to pass small fishing skiffs, and speeding through open sweeps of water, was Ralph's idea of the only way to live.

The contrast between Tarzan and Mr. McKay was amazing, and one always wondered what possible bond between the two men had made them so inseparable. One was never seen without the other; their lives seemed to be inextricably woven together.

McKay was a small man, almost delicate in a lean, small-boned way. Tarzan was an enormous man, tall, wide-shouldered and long-armed, with the smoothly flowing muscles and easy movements of a sinuous snake. There was something snake-like in the ease and motion of his body, arms and legs. And his features added to that reptilian look. His head had the flat look of an adder. A receding hairline at both temples of his pale crew-cut hair emphasized the triangular shape of his head. His mouth was wide and lipless. When he dropped his lower jaw to grunt a sullen monosyllable, Tarzan's face resembled an alert and impatient alligator ready to swallow anything alive in sight. His eyes were a pale, almost colorless blue, heavy-lidded and sullen, and his ears were small and set close to his head. His chest, arms and legs were slick and yellowish, without any hair whatsoever. As he stepped down from the upper level of the cruiser to grunt his recognition of Maria's presence, she instinctively moved away from him.

"Ralph's girl, huh?" he said expressionlessly, thrusting out his lower jaw.

"No," Maria replied, instantly resentful. "Just on a date, that's all."

Without another word, Tarzan lowered a hooded lid in McKay's direction, nodded twice, and turned away. He wiped his oily hands on his bare chest and made his way forward. Dropping bonelessly to the deck he stretched out to his full length, arms above his head, and lay on his back to sun himself.

"And that's my crew, Maria," McKay said. "Tarzan is what we call him, and if he has any other name he hasn't got around to telling me yet. But then," he added with an amused smile, "I've only known him for ten years."

"He frightens me," Maria said simply.

McKay laughed. "He's as gentle as a child, my dear. And I'd trust him with my life. In fact I do. He's my paid male companion, my close friend, my chauffeur and bodyguard."

"Why do you need a bodyguard? Are you mixed up with unions

or something?" Maria had never known a man who employed a bodyguard.

"No." McKay shook his head and smiled. "I have money, Maria, a great amount of money, and sometimes I carry a bit of it with me. Tarzan's presence ensures that I keep it."

"Oh! I see," Maria said, but she didn't really understand why a cultured gentleman like Mr. McKay would keep a crumb like Tarzan around for five minutes. She knew she wouldn't!

Ralph was now in the open bay and he had raised the speed to twenty-five knots. The dark blue water was choppy and the prow slapped up and down as it split the sea. Over the powerful diesel engine's roar conversation was difficult. Maria changed her seat and sat down in one of the comfortable fishing chairs facing the wide, boiling wake. They had been out on the water for almost an hour and Maria was getting stiff and a little bored by the ride. McKay sat in the other fishing chair beside her puffing a briar pipe which he relit every few moments with a jet-fed pipe lighter.

"Would you like to fish, my dear?" McKay asked Maria, sensing her growing boredom.

"Gee, Captain," she replied, "I don't know. I've never fished in my life!"

"Why not try it then?" Mr. McKay left his seat, tapped Ralph on the shoulder and told him to move the craft in slow wide circles, and stay in the center of the bay. Ralph cut the speed down to three knots and the boat rocked gently with incoming swells from the open sea. He set and held the wheel for a gradual graceful curve.

McKay removed a short plastic rod-and-reel from the seat locker on the port side, and a moment later was showing Maria how to cast and how to handle the reel. To demonstrate he stood behind her, pressing his pelvis tightly against her full buttocks, and also found it necessary to put his arms around her with his hands over hers upon the reel. Ralph didn't relish the slow speed of the boat and the effortless steering, and he disliked how Mr. McKay was giving Maria instructions. He wanted to yell through the open windshield for Tarzan to take the wheel, but the bodyguard was evidently asleep, and he didn't have any legitimate reason to awaken the man.

Maria was having fun. After she got the general gist of casting and tried it clumsily a few times, she decided she could cast without any help from Mr. McKay. She had been so intent on the rod-and-reel she hadn't noticed the tightness of McKay's insistent pressure against her buttocks, but as she wiggled a couple of times to break away from his embrace in an easy manner—after all, she didn't want to offend the old gentleman—she became highly aware of what that pressure meant. Again she waggled her full hips to break away, but Mr. McKay only held her tighter than before. Maria had been trapped in similar situations at high school dances, and had felt this same kind of pressure against the flesh of her thigh as some pimply-faced kid had held her tightly and against her will. She had known how to handle high school boys. But what could she do when the man was so gentlemanly, and talked about casting all the time in a calm, even voice as though nothing were wrong? For two cents she would have slapped Mr. McKay's face, but he acted so innocent about everything—and yet he was holding her more tightly than before!

"I don't believe I like to fish!" Maria said sharply. She jerked away from McKay, and tossed the rod-and-reel to the deck. His expressionless face was flushed and his eyes were bright. McKay picked up the rod and began to wind the fishing cord noisily onto the reel. There was a gentle smile on his face.

"I find fishing very relaxing myself," he said blandly. "But it takes a long time to become an expert. Would you like some lunch?" Without waiting for her reply, McKay called forward, "Tarzan!"

With what seemed to be but a single bound Tarzan was roused from his slumbers and was standing at slouched attention on the deck in front of Mr. McKay. The boat owner handed Tarzan the rod-and-reel to put away, and told him to bring lunch.

"Perhaps you would like a swim before you eat, Maria?" McKay said. "There are no sharks out here, I assure you."

"I didn't bring my suit," the girl replied.

"There are some in the cabin. I believe one of them would fit you."

"Oh, I could never wear another person's bathing suit!"

"All right," McKay said, with a shrug of indifference. "How about you, Ralph? Would you like a swim?"

"I didn't bring any trunks either, Mr. McKay, but I'm more interested in food than swimming."

There was a splash as Tarzan dived into the water in his dirty duck trousers. The others watched for a moment, as Tarzan swam out across the gently swelling sea with powerful motions of his arms and shoulders, and then they turned to the food with gusto. Ralph, who had been half-starved ever since coming to Miami Beach, could scarcely conceal his greed as he dropped a canful of tiny succulent Norwegian sardines down his throat, two at a time. There were thick ragged slices of fresh rye bread with the crusts cut away, and Ralph made a Lucullan sandwich of beaded, yellow Swiss cheese, a layer of tender salami, three bright-red and juicy slices of tomato, a half-dozen circles of sliced dill pickle, liverwurst, a thick slice of shimmering Spanish onion, topping the contents off with a huge spoonful of hot mustard. He slapped another piece of bread on top with a crushing movement, blending the ingredients into an incredible mixture of sheer delight.

McKay poured out three glassfuls of Moselle from the tall, narrow-necked bottle into fragile glasses, and winked humorously at Maria. "Perhaps I should have brought another basket?"

He was obviously joking; there was enough food in the wicker hamper to feed ten hungry people.

"It's all so *good!*" Maria exclaimed.

Maria had filled an enamelware plate with generous bits of chopped cold pork, large slivers from three different cheeses, and had added a heaping portion of potato salad.

Maria enjoyed the novelty of the cold wine. McKay, playing the host, picked here and there at the assortment, but mainly contented himself with watching the other two and keeping their glasses filled. Ralph could not remember a day in his life more perfect than that afternoon. He ate until he could eat no more, and then sipped sleepily at the Moselle, relishing its sunny flavor. He looked often at Maria, admiring her beauty, wondering vaguely how he could manage a night date with her before she returned to the North and left his life forever...

Maria had forgotten her momentary flash of anger at Mr. McKay, dismissing the event as a product of her imagination, justifying his goat-like actions by telling herself that he had had a penknife or a fountain pen in his trousers pocket.

Mr. McKay leaned forward, placed a small hand lightly on her knee, and frowned as he examined her face for a long moment.

"What's the matter?" Maria asked.

"You're getting too much sun, young lady. I think we'd better go in."

The breeze across the water and the sea itself made them feel as if their position in the middle of the bay was at least fifteen degrees cooler than it was ashore. But the heat of the Florida sun had not changed. Maria put fingers to her face.

"I think my face is too hot," she said anxiously. "And I do burn, with my light complexion and all."

"We don't want that, do we?" Mr. McKay said with a kind and considerate smile. He turned his head and shouted: "Tarzan! Take us in!"

A few minutes later, Tarzan at the helm, the craft moved slowly across the bay toward the Marina and its berth.

Maria had marveled at the efficiency and ease with which Tarzan, without a helping hand, put away the luncheon objects, folded the table and raised the anchors and the swimming ladder. Not a motion was wasted; he slithered past each task and when you looked again it was accomplished. Maria still disliked him, and when he once turned his cold, blue eyes on her face, staring blankly from beneath thickly-hooded lids, a cold shiver of fear ran down her back.

At the dock, Tarzan leaped lightly to the pier and secured the craft forward, while Ralph took care of the aft lines. Ralph jumped back on the sunken deck and smiled ingratiatingly at Mr. McKay.

"I don't know when I've had a nicer day, Mr. McKay," Ralph said. "I really had a wonderful time, and I appreciate you letting me bring Maria along—"

"I want to thank you very, very much, too," Maria broke in sincerely.

"Now wait a minute!" Mr. McKay held up his hand. "It's only three-thirty, and I have an idea. Suppose all of us run the *Sea Witch* up along the inland waterway as far as Fort Lauderdale. We can have a decent dinner there, and then come back tonight. I promise to get you back to the dock by one A.M. at the latest. What do you say?"

Ralph frowned. "I'd love to Mr. McKay, but I've got to be at work at eight."

"That poses a problem." McKay pursed his lips. "But what about Maria, now? She's on a vacation. A trip along the waterway would be a grand experience for her." He laughed pleasantly. And then earnestly: "I know you'll enjoy it, Maria. If you're only in Florida for one week you really should see as much as you can."

Maria looked down at her bare legs, shorts and sandals. "I'm a mess, Captain McKay, I can't go anywhere to eat like this!" she wailed.

"You don't have to," McKay assured her. "I'll call ahead to the *maitre d'* at the Robert Fulton and order dinner. He owes me a few favors, and I'll have dinner served out here on deck. Now what would be an appropriate dinner for a night when the moon is full in Florida...?" Closing his eyes and walking restlessly away from the young couple, his hands clasped behind his back, McKay moved his lips silently as he turned this perplexing problem over in his mind.

Almost too late, Maria remembered that she was on a date with Ralph. Stricken, she looked into his eyes. "Gosh, Ralph," she said. "I'm really on a date with you! And we have the rest of the afternoon and all..." her tremulous voice faded.

Ralph shook his head. "Forget that part, Maria. I didn't have any exact plans and I have to work tonight anyway. What else would you do tonight? Hang around the Rotunda Room? Go ahead. You'll have a good time, and I'll tell your roommate, Miss Vittorni, not to expect you till late."

"Would you do that for me? Would you please?" Maria exclaimed eagerly, clasping Ralph's wrist with a small firm grip. "You don't really mind, do you, Ralph?"

Ralph smiled pleasantly. What a bust I must be, he thought. She acts as happy as if I released her foot from a bear trap or something. "No," Ralph said again. "You go ahead, Maria. It'll be a nice trip for you and I know you'll enjoy it."

"Thanks, Ralph. Something like this boat is really a different experience for a city girl."

Ralph thanked Mr. McKay again for the afternoon, left the pier and returned to his car. As soon as he slid behind the wheel and lit a cigarette, a deep, dark gloom settled over his mind. He remembered that Donald McKay was one of the main owners of the Rotunda Hotel. If he had really wanted Ralph to go along, all he had to do was lift the telephone at the end of the pier, call the manager and order him to replace Ralph at the elevator for the night. Just like that, he could have done it, Ralph thought bitterly.

"The sonofabitch!" Ralph said aloud. "The dirty, rich sonofabitch!"

FIVE

THE *Sea Witch* glided slowly through the deep mid-channel of the placid inland waterway toward Lauderdale, chugging softly at reduced speed. Maria, from her soft chair on the wide after-well deck, admired the beautiful homes, and waved to the fishermen on the numberless bridges. When the channel paralleled the highway for long stretches, she stared back boldly at the passengers in passing automobiles who ogled the white, expensive cabin cruiser.

"Every one of these people envies me," she mused, "and who can blame them? They think I'm rich, and I feel rich on this boat. I feel as though I were born for this life, and that I've been cheated somehow out of an inheritance..."

Mr. McKay opened the door from the cabin below, and approached Maria with a tall Tom Collins in his hand. This was the drink Maria had ordered, and she smiled her thanks and sipped it gratefully. The gin taste was strong and good, unlike the Collinses served in the Rotunda Room.

"This is wonderful, Mr. McKay. Aren't you going to have one?"

"Later, my dear. My doctor has limited me to three drinks a day, so I usually save all three for the evening and drink them all at once."

"Isn't that cheating?" Maria laughed.

"No, I call it subterfuge. Look over there," McKay pointed. "That's going to be a new cooperative apartment house. I own a big piece of it."

Maria's eyes followed his pointing finger, and she examined the eight-story mass of raw, unpainted concrete. Without their glass panes the black and gaping windows looked like mouse-holes in the concrete façade, but already Maria could see the underlying design of the modern structure to come.

"Cooperative apartments? That's where everybody buys their own apartment, like a house?"

"That's right. These apartments cost thirty-five thousand apiece, and there'll be a maintenance fee of one hundred and fifty dollars a month, as well."

"Thirty-five thousand! For an apartment? How many rooms do they get for that?"

"Two bedrooms. And a fairly large living room. Of course, there isn't any dining room and they have to eat their meals in the living room."

"Is anybody crazy enough to pay that much money for a two-bedroom apartment, and then pay a monthly maintenance fee besides?" Maria said indignantly.

"Certainly, my dear!" McKay's eyes slanted with amusement at the girl's naiveté.

"You won't get that much," Maria said positively, setting her glass on the deck and crossing her arms. "You'll lose your shirt; that's what's going to happen to you!"

McKay chuckled quietly. "No, Maria, I won't lose any money. All of the apartments were sold before we even broke the ground."

"I can't believe it!" the girl exclaimed. "Why we only pay seventy-five a month rent for three bedrooms on the East Side."

"The East Side, in New York, is not the Gold Coast in Southern Florida, my dear. People who live here have plenty of money, and in New York, as you should know, your monthly rent would be considerably higher if you lived on Park Avenue."

"It's still a lot of money," she said, "just for two bedrooms."

"Not really," Mr. McKay replied conversationally. "Take my boat, for instance. It will sleep four, six in a pinch, but for all general purposes, there is only one large room, the saloon; a small galley, and a bathroom."

"A boat is different."

"Well, then, how much do you think I paid for the *Sea Witch*?"

Maria looked about the deck, her eyes shifting from the mahogany rails to the deep leather seats circling the deck, to the high fishing riggers, back to the aluminum fishing chairs with their deep, soft cushions, then again to the highly-polished pieces of brass almost everywhere she looked, and she was unable to make an educated guess.

"I just don't know, Captain McKay." She hesitated. "But it cost you a lot, I know. Overestimating for fun, I'll say twenty thousand."

"I was cheated then." McKay patted Maria kindly on her shoulder. "Seventy-five thousand, in ice-cold cash. But I bought it new," he teased, "instead of second hand."

Maria picked up her drink from the deck, jiggled the ice for a moment, and then shook her dark curls. "Maybe I'd better shut up," she said with a little laugh. "I don't know what I'm talking about."

Tarzan pushed the horn three times for a drawbridge. McKay and Maria were silent until the boat passed through the opening and the bridge dropped down behind them.

"Somehow, Captain," Maria said petulantly, "all this isn't right. I work like hell all year long—pardon my French—but I really do! I save all year, scrimping on things I sometimes really need, just to take a week's vacation. And yet there are people who can afford to buy those expensive apartments, or stay in Miami Beach hotels for months and months in rooms costing fifty and seventy-five dollars a day! Where do they get all this money? I work like hell for mine, and they only pay me fifty dollars a week!" Maria was close to tears.

"That's America, Maria," McKay said soothingly. "Free enterprise under the capitalistic system, and it's the best system in the world. I started out with an inheritance of four Negro houses in Jacksonville, and I made mine in real estate. Now, I know a thousand ways to make money. Maybe, if you're interested, I'll tell you a few ways you can earn money. Tonight, after dinner."

"Why not tell me now?"

"Because I feel like taking a nap. If you want another drink, I made a pitcher of Collinses, and they're on the table downstairs. You know where the cigarettes are, so help yourself. Enjoy the ride, and don't worry about anything."

"I'm not a child!" Maria snapped. "I got mad, that's all. Anybody with any sense gets mad when they see injustice staring them in the face!"

"Cool off, Irish," McKay laughed. "Consider your good points. You've got at least two, I know!"

"Oh, don't mind me," Maria said good-naturedly. "I'm always flying off the handle. Go ahead and take a nap. I'll be all right."

But after McKay had disappeared below, Maria still pondered the tedium of her life. How could it possibly be right to work all the time at a stupid job without any hope of bettering her position? She could—perhaps—quit work if she married Sidney Halper. What improvement would that be? He was now only a small cog in management, but in time, he would have a good paying job. At present he was in charge of the company show room. It sounded terrific, but all he did was keep the place straightened out, putting bolts of cloth back in their bins, or dragging out material samples for buyers visiting New York. And his take-home pay was only $87.50 a week, not a great deal more than her own. To make the money stretch, he would probably expect her to continue working, even if they did get married. What with expenses as they were today, she might never be able to quit work if she married Sidney.

Oh, damnit! Maria thought. I'm every bit as attractive as these rich women riding around in powder-blue convertibles in Miami Beach. They weren't any smarter, or even as beautiful as I am, some of them, with their dark glasses and long cigarette holders! Why should they be the ones to live in $35,000 apartments with ease and luxury and drive around with nothing to do, and a silly pink French poodle yapping in the front seat? Why? Why? Why?

The sky was quite dark by the time the *Sea Witch* reached the canals of Fort Lauderdale. Tarzan expertly steered the boat into a dark canal which shortly came to a dead end at a wide expanse of lawn bordering a rambling, aluminum-shuttered residence. There was a small pier jutting out from the lawn. Tarzan shut off the engines, leaped swiftly to the pier and snubbed the lines fore and aft. Tarzan found a switch for the pier lights and flooded the mooring and boat with overhead brilliance. He pulled a long black cord out from the side of the boat, plugged it into a socket on the pier, and the air-conditioner inside the cabin began to hum. Then, without a backward glance, he ran lightly across the lawn and disappeared into the darkness.

McKay came on deck, and Maria's mouth dropped open in surprise. He had changed into summer evening dress. There was a dark red carnation in the lapel of his white linen jacket. He wore slim black pumps, with narrow bows of yellow plaid, and the predominantly yellow tartan was repeated in his bow-tie and cummerbund.

"You aren't fair!" Maria said angrily. "Here you are, all dressed up, and I'm wearing shorts and a man's white shirt."

"Now don't get your temper up again." McKay glanced at his wristwatch. "It'll be some time before dinner, so why don't you, like a good little girl, go below and take a shower, and then see what you can find to wear down there. All right?"

"All right," Maria replied sullenly. She felt cheated. She was in a party mood without a party dress.

Already the air-conditioner had cooled the saloon, and Maria stepped into the lower temperature gratefully. She went to the cramped little bathroom and took a shower. After drying her glowing body with a huge monogrammed towel, Maria reentered the luxurious cabin, holding the towel about her, and began to explore the various closets. She didn't find women's evening clothes as she expected, but she did discover a long black nylon nightgown and its matching black flowing negligee, with filmy, puffed sleeves, lacy, ruffled wrists and collar.

I suppose these are what he had in mind, she reflected grimly, but I'll fool him and wear them...over my shorts! She slipped into her panties and red shorts, but hesitated when she picked up her brassiere. No, she mused, I'll give the old codger a break and play fair with him. I won't wear the brassiere. He won't be able to see them too well anyway, with two layers of black nylon over them, but he's entitled to something for this wonderful afternoon and dinner.

The nightgown was a size thirty-four, and Maria found that she could get into it without too much difficulty, although she would have preferred a thirty-six. She adjusted her heavy breasts comfortably beneath the gown, slipped her arms into the negligee and tied the filmy matching nylon belt about her narrow waist. She returned to the bathroom and put on fresh red lips with lipstick. After a frowning examination of her complexion, staring intently at the well-lighted mirror, Maria felt that she would "do."

She stepped away from the glass, threw her shoulders back and stiffened her spine. She stood erect with her sandalled feet close together. The firm outline of her full breasts could be clearly seen through the thin transparent material. Maria smiled at her reflection in the mirror and thought maybe Mr. McKay will get a thrill for himself.

And then, with sudden terror, she remembered Tarzan and the

cold, cruel blue of his eyes. Without thinking, Maria hurriedly stripped off the negligee and gown and squirmed quickly into the scanty protection of her brassiere. Again she donned the black nightgown and flowing robe, and with a defiant shake of her black curls, climbed the ladder to the deck.

Maria had never had such a dinner before in her life. A small table had been set up on deck with a bowl of white gardenias in the center. The *maitre d'* of the Robert Fulton Hotel, with the assistance of two waiters, personally served all courses. There was a different wine with each course, and Maria was able to drink the wine, but unable to eat much dinner. There was too much of everything, and besides, she watched McKay and tried to eat only what he did. McKay wasn't a heavy eater, so many of the toothsome items were picked over and then removed after a suitable period by the *maitre d'*. McKay was a charming dinner companion and answered all of Maria's questions about money with an amused air of quiet assurance.

She was unable to comprehend how so many people in Florida had made so much money. McKay finally got it through her pretty head.

"It isn't really difficult, once you understand, Maria," he told her patiently. "There are thousands of very small towns in the United States, not counting the cities and their rich industrialists. In every small town there are one or two men who are well off. They own a small local factory, or perhaps large land holdings farmed on a big scale. Just one or two such men in every town. They work hard, and their money gradually piles up in the bank. One day they sit back, look around, and wake up. They are rich, and finally realize it. So they sell out and quit, thinking that they've worked hard and long enough, and move to California or Florida. Having lived fairly frugally all their lives, they splurge. These are the people who make up the wealthy majority here. Do you see?"

"But what about all these women I see, driving around in convertibles? Where do they get all their money?"

"From the rich men, of course." McKay smiled easily. "A lot of their wives don't like it down here. They miss friends, children, grandchildren and their homes. So they go back. But the husband stays. He finds himself a mistress, and the young woman takes him for all she can get, which is plenty. But so what? Now he can afford it, and he can't take it with him, you know."

"I see. But it all sounds so immoral."

"Morality and money are not synonymous. A man who becomes rich has always obtained his money through immorality. If he had a small town factory he became rich by cheating his workers. If he worked large land holdings, he forced out the small farmers and paid low wages. His front was phoney in the small town, but down here on the Gold Coast, a rich man can get away with anything. His immorality no longer has to be kept under cover, so he lets himself go."

"You certainly have opened my eyes, Mr. McKay."

McKay snapped his fingers at the fawning *maitre d'*. "Clear all this away and take the champagne below," he ordered.

"Yes, sir."

"I think we'll be more comfortable in the saloon, Maria, with the air-conditioner."

"What about Tarzan?" Maria whispered softly.

Tarzan sat cross-legged on the dock, eating from a brown paper sack full of hamburgers and drinking great swigs of milk from a cardboard container.

"He'll stay on the dock," McKay shrugged. "He could have eaten with us, you know. And there is plenty left over, for that matter. He prefers hamburgers and milk. Rich food doesn't agree with Tarzan."

McKay helped Maria to her feet. She staggered slightly, and almost fell.

"I'm beginning to feel all that wine," she giggled.

"You'll feel better where it's cool. We can taper off on the champagne." The *maitre d'* held the cabin door open. McKay steadied Maria as she gingerly felt for the steps with her toe. The head waiter softly closed the door behind him, after leaving the champagne.

Maria was beginning to feel somewhat dizzy, and sat down immediately on the soft double bed. She watched McKay with bright eyes as he slowly worked the cork out of the magnum of champagne. When the cork flew out the bubbling wine was poured into two wide glasses. She laughed delightedly.

"This is the way to live, Captain," Maria said gaily as she accepted her glass. "I never want to go back to New York!"

"Perhaps you won't have to go back." He touched her glass with his, and before drinking, made a smiling toast. "To your virginity."

"I'll drink to that," Maria laughed, and drained her glass. She held her glass for a refill, and peered owlishly at McKay. "You might think I'm kidding, Captain, but I am a virgin!"

"But I do believe you, my dear." McKay set his brimming glass down on the table. "How much did your week's vacation cost you, Maria?"

"It isn't over yet," she laughed. "Five dollars a week for fifty weeks. I saved five dollars every single week out of my pay. You figure it out."

McKay removed an ostrich-skin wallet from his hip pocket. As Maria watched him with mounting excitement, he removed twelve crisp twenty-dollar bills from the wallet, counted them twice, hesitated for a second, and then added one more twenty to the stack. He folded the sheaf of money once, and dropped the sum into Maria's straw handbag.

"What's that for?" Maria sat up as straight as she could and focused her eyes on McKay's impassive face.

"For you." McKay shrugged comically. "If you want it. Two hundred and sixty dollars. A year of savings for a week in Miami. Or if you look at it another way, about five weeks of office work for your firm. But you can have the same amount of money for a few moments of pleasant relaxation."

"Why don't you come right out and say what you mean?" Maria said sharply. "Although I know exactly what you mean! I'm not that kind of girl, and you know it, Mr. McKay!" Maria got shakily to her feet.

"Suit yourself, Maria," McKay said indifferently. "I'm a man who always pays for what I want. And I usually get what I want. But I don't argue price, and I don't haggle. I believe the sum is enough, and there's no point in trying to raise the ante."

"You don't understand, Mr. McKay!" Maria cried indignantly. "You've got my words confused or something. I wasn't trying to raise the price or anything like that. There isn't any price on my virginity!" She shook her head as if to clear it. "Now I'm getting

all mixed up. Pour me some more champagne and let me explain."
She sat down again, and pounded her knee with a small fist.

"All right." McKay filled her empty glass, which Maria tried
to drink all at once. Most of the wine spilled down her chin and
splashed sloppily on her gown.

"Now I've spilled it," she wailed childishly. "You've got to give
me more!"

McKay patiently refilled her glass, replaced the bottle in the
silver bucket, and sat beside Maria on the bed. He placed an arm
around her waist and kissed her on the neck. His lips then kissed
the hollow between her breasts. With his tongue, he licked at the
spilled champagne beneath the collar of Maria's nightgown. She
pushed him firmly away with one hand, holding the full glass
carefully with the other.

"All right." McKay sipped from his glass and got to his feet. He
half sat on the table and took off his jacket, tie, and shirt as Maria
talked. His eyes were wet and glistening and his fingers trembled.

"What I mean to say, Captain McKay," Maria hesitated, slowly
gathering her confused thoughts, "is this! I'm just along for the
boat ride. That's all. My body—" she looked down at her full
breasts fondly—"isn't for sale. Not for any old two hundred and
sixty dollars or anything else. I'm not selling and I'm not buying." She liked the sound of the last sentence, and she repeated
it. "I'm not selling, and I'm not buying! I'm sorry," she shrugged
and took another long sip from her glass, "but that's the way it
is. Understand?" She peered up at McKay's face to see if she had
made her position clear.

"I understand." McKay removed a yellow silk dressing gown
from the closet, and slipped his thin arms into the sleeves. "So I'll
take back my money." McKay picked up Maria's bag, removed
the crisp sheaf of bills and counted it moving his lips silently.

"Leave it!" In Maria's voice there was a sudden mixture of wea-
riness, regret, and a certain coarseness that had never been there
before. If she could have heard it, she would have denied the voice
as her own.

McKay dropped the money inside the bag, took Maria's empty
glass from her nerveless fingers, and placed it on the table. The girl
was completely aware of what followed, but her body was almost
helpless, without life of its own. McKay methodically removed

Maria's clothing, the way a mother undresses a child. Undressed and lying flat on her back, Maria rolled her head nervously. McKay kissed her soft lips, but she didn't respond.

"You won't hurt me, will you?" She began to cry drunkenly. McKay patted her bare shoulder reassuringly, and she stopped crying immediately, wiped her streaming eyes with the back of her hand. "I'm sorry," she said contritely. "I just don't know anything, Captain McKay. I don't know how to help you or anything, I'm so dumb."

"Don't talk," McKay said. "Don't say anything."

Maria fixed her eyes on the ceiling and put her hands behind her head. At first she was surprised, almost stunned by Mr. McKay's actions, but the instant of shock changed to amusement and she found it difficult to suppress a fit of drunken giggling.

"Is that all he wanted to do for that money?" she thought with wonder. "Why that's kid stuff! That's what Peggy and I used to do three or four years ago!"

The dark panelling of the ceiling began to spin and Maria tightly closed her eyes. Her hands clutched the sheets convulsively, and the room still spun crazily inside her head. A moment later the spinning stopped as suddenly as it had begun, and she drifted down into deep, contented sleep.

SIX

THE brilliant sunlight reflecting from the white concrete driveway in front of the Rotunda Hotel stung Ralph's eyes, and he rubbed them hard with the heels of his palms. He blinked rapidly, and then lifted his eyes to the tops of the green palms bordering the highway to rest them. Leaning against the pink concrete wall of the hotel, a few paces away from the wide, glass entrance door, he waited impatiently for Maria. The time was now eight A.M., and he had held his uncomfortable post for two hours. He felt like he had been waiting there for days.

More than thirty-eight hours had passed since Ralph had any sleep, and his eyelids were granulated and sore. From his knees down Ralph's legs and feet were almost numb, and there was a throbbing, painful beat inside his kidneys. And still Maria had not returned. But he wouldn't leave without talking to her, so he held his position and waited.

Why Maria really mattered to him, he didn't know. All night he had tried to figure out the answer to that one with no success. He only knew that she did matter, that Maria was the most wonderful girl he had ever met in his life. Whether it was love, or whether it was only a fierce and wholesome sexual attraction, he didn't know. They had gotten along well together on their morning date; Maria had apparently enjoyed listening to him talk about himself, and he had been equally interested in her observations. Not that there had been any world-shaking conversation, or anything like that; he couldn't remember much of what they had talked about, for that matter.

But all night long, riding up and down in the elevator, Ralph had pondered his feelings, worrying every scrap of conversation he could recall, every action of the day, like a dog worrying a bone. He tried to minimize his relationship with her—which he grudgingly admitted was only a casual date, no matter how his mind tried to magnify the relationship—but she began to loom even larger in his mind; a perfect, flawless, incomparable beauty. In fact, everything that any man could ever want in a woman! And he had been too stupid to see it all day because of her very closeness!

As the night wore away, and six A.M. approached, his mind was unrealistically fevered. Ralph began to see Rich Man McKay, and Poor Girl Maria, in a sordid series of dirty pictures...the sweet, innocent girl succumbing to a depraved old man's desires, doing anything the rich man wanted her to do. In his maddened state, Ralph vividly envisioned a great many things McKay would want Maria to do. And what was worse, he saw Maria doing them.

After Johnny Townsend relieved him at the elevator, Ralph still couldn't go home, not until he had seen Maria. He wanted to see for himself if what he had pictured in his mind had actually happened. How he would know by merely seeing and talking to the girl he didn't know. He only knew he had to wait and see.

Too little sleep, too many dexedrine tablets, too little money, furious anger at McKay for taking Maria away from him, and morose brooding throughout a long and boring night had turned Ralph Tone into a highly irrational person.

With his eyes closed to angry slits and with his confused mind churning, Ralph failed to see Tarzan and McKay drop Maria off at the curb. Maria waved goodbye to McKay as Tarzan whipped the yellow Cadillac back into the traffic stream. She turned and strolled slowly up the curving, concrete driveway. Maria saw Ralph first, and hailed him.

"Morning, Ralph!" she called cheerfully. "Getting some sun?"

Ralph's eyelids flew open, and he bounced off the wall like a handball. With three quick strides he faced Maria, reached out and gripped her wrist with steely fingers. His color was a deep, angry red, and his red-rimmed eyes glared into the girl's frightened face.

"Where have you been all night, damn you?" He spat the words out accusingly.

"Let me go, Ralph!" Maria said fearfully. "You're hurting my wrist!"

Ralph immediately released Maria's slim wrist, and ran his fingers through his hair. "I knew it!" Ralph said angrily. He stepped back two paces and appraised Maria's full figure for a brief moment, shaking his head unbelievingly. Maria, of course, was dressed exactly as she had been the morning before, but under Ralph's close scrutiny her face flushed, and her temper flared.

"Knew what?" she cried angrily.

Ralph nodded his chin knowingly, sneered at the girl, and then reversed the motion of his head and shook it from side to side. With unreasoning hatred he stared into Maria's angry, apprehensive eyes.

"Just tell me one thing," he said bitterly, running his fingers nervously through his crinkly hair again. "Just one thing! That's all I want to know. How much did he have to pay you? That's all I want to know."

Maria visibly paled, and her full mouth quivered. Impulsively she hugged her straw handbag to her stomach, and hot tears welled out of her brown eyes. She made a blubbering, whimpering sound deep in her throat, pressed a tight fist to her open mouth and ran past Ralph to the hotel entrance.

Filled with sudden remorse, Ralph started after her, but stopped before he reached the entrance.

"What's the use," he thought ruefully. "After an insult like that, she'd never forgive me in a million years."

Ralph's heart was a heavy weight inside his chest as he drove home to his rooming house. Too late for breakfast, he showered and stretched out naked on top of his unmade bed. There was nothing left to do now but apologize to the girl—that is, if she would let him talk to her. If she didn't he couldn't blame her. Although he thought he would never be able to sleep again, within a few minutes his fatigued body took over and he fell asleep.

At two P.M. Tommy Grant entered the room and began to bang dresser drawers in and out noisily, whistle loudly off-key and bump against the foot of the bed. Tommy was on his afternoon break, and wanted somebody to talk to. After a few minutes, the racket awakened Ralph and he sat up groggily on the edge of the bed.

"Why don't you beat on a couple of boilers?" he growled at his roommate.

"Did I wake you?" Tommy lifted his eyebrows with feigned surprise. "I'm sorry, Ralph."

"That's all right. Give me a cigarette."

Tommy lit a cigarette and handed it to Ralph. Ralph shook his head to clear away a clinging drowsiness, and gratefully sucked smoke deep into his lungs.

"How'd you make out with the chick from the hotel, Ralph?"

Tommy asked, a wide grin on his cheerful face.

Ralph groaned. "Don't remind me!" He shook his head with swiftly-remembered despair. "I made an ass out of myself, that's all. Never in my life have I pulled such a stupid stunt. To tell you the truth, Tommy, I'm so ashamed of myself, I'm ready to quit my job and never go back to the hotel. Just to face Maria again after what I said to her is unbearable to even think about."

Tommy had only asked an innocent question, but now he was concerned about his friend. "It can't be that bad, Ralph," he said. "Tell me about it."

Ralph cut a few corners in the rehash of events, but the uneven story was true enough. He had fallen hard for Maria, and he didn't know why. McKay had taken her away from him and she hadn't returned to the hotel until after eight that morning. As a consequence he had expected the worst and accused her of it. He related the scene in front of the hotel with self-punishing detail.

Tommy had listened quietly and now he looked thoughtfully at his friend. "You may not be so crazy, Ralph," he said softly. "And don't get sore at me, either. But I know a few things about this guy McKay. Or at least I've heard a few things even if I don't know whether they're all true or not."

"What do you mean, 'things'?" Ralph asked sharply.

"Rumors, I suppose." Tommy shrugged his shoulders. "I can't prove anything. I don't know anything about this girl. I've noticed her, because she stands out like a flower in a bunch of ragweed. But you don't know a damn thing about her and neither do I. Suppose she made up that story? Do you actually know she's a typist in New York, and down here only for a vacation?"

"I know something about people, Tommy," Ralph said defensively. "If she made up the things she told me she'd have to be a damned good actress."

"Maybe so," Tommy nodded. "But you don't know. Right?"

"I suppose."

"What about McKay then? You've taken girls up to his penthouse, and some of them stay all night. Right?"

"I know that, all right!" Ralph said bitterly. "That's why I got suspicious when Maria didn't show up until this morning. If she'd come back around one A.M. or something like that, I probably wouldn't have thought anything about it."

"Let me talk, Ralph. Do you remember that guy Bruno, used to be a waiter, then quit to go up to Palm Beach?"

"I saw him in the locker room a few times. But I didn't know him."

"Well, I talked to him a lot. Mr. McKay hired Bruno one night to serve dinner and mix drinks out at his house near the 'Glades. You knew about his house, didn't you?"

"Yeah. Go on."

"Bruno didn't tell me what all happened, but he kind of hinted. There were eight men there, and Bruno said I'd be shocked if he mentioned a couple of the names. Anyway, there was a real fancy dinner, and afterwards, movies in the living room. Stag movies. Bruno tended bar, and got to watch the movies. He said they were really something to see, boy, strictly stag! Now, here's something funny—all the men called each other Mr. Smith. They laughed about it, but they all called each other Mr. Smith. After the movies were all over, about a half-dozen girls arrived. The houseboy and McKay's bodyguard let them in, and they went directly to the bedrooms, not the living room. McKay made an announcement that the show would begin in a few minutes; there was another rush to the bar, and then McKay sent Bruno home. Bruno said he didn't see the 'show,' but I think he was lying. Anyway, McKay gave him a hundred bucks. A hell of a lot of dough for only serving dinner and mixing a few drinks."

"Not really. Not for eight or nine people. But what kind of show?"

"What do you think, Ralph? You know damned well what kind of a show it was!"

"Well, so what?"

"I'm not saying Maria is one of the party girls, but McKay has to get girls from somewhere, don't he? And if she isn't, why wouldn't he try to recruit her? See what I mean?"

Ralph set his jaw, got to his feet, and began to dress. "I'm going down to the Marina and talk to that McKay," he said grimly.

"What for? Bruno might've been lying through his teeth. And what can you say to Mr. McKay anyway, Ralph? You can't prove anything."

"I'm going to come right out and ask him. If he lies I'll be able to tell it, and then I'll knock his teeth down his throat!"

"What about his bodyguard?"

"Tarzan? I don't like him either. I'd like to break his yellow, slimy jaw while I'm at it."

"Don't go, Ralph!" Tommy pleaded. "You'll only get into a lot of trouble and lose your job besides!"

Ralph didn't reply, and hurried down the stairs.

However, on the drive to the Marina, Ralph cooled off considerably. The more he thought about the story, the more unlikely the waiter's tale seemed to be. McKay had been pretty damned nice to Ralph, and a guy couldn't fake friendliness. There was no reason for it. In spite of being rich he had treated Ralph as an equal. And up until yesterday afternoon, Ralph had thought McKay a terrific guy. If it hadn't been for Maria, he would still think so. Bruno's story must be just a jealous fabrication made up out of whole cloth, a vicious story. So McKay had a girl up to his penthouse once in a while. So what? He was rich and single, and he was entitled to have an occasional girl, wasn't he? But to accuse McKay of procuring girls and running orgies for famous men was ridiculous! Why should he? He had more dough now than he could use.

Ralph eased into a slanted parking slot at the Marina and sat indecisively in his car. A few hours sleep certainly made a difference in your thinking ability. Ralph grinned ruefully. Well, as long as he was here, he could say hello to Mr. McKay, anyway.

The *Sea Witch* was in her slip, and McKay was seated at a table on the after-well deck in the sun. A chess board was before him and he was intently studying a chess problem in an opened book. He read silently for a moment with a furrowed brow, shook his head impatiently and then hesitantly moved a black Queen's Pawn. Tarzan was forward, sprawled out on the deck, reading a comic book. He raised his head and stared expressionlessly at Ralph, and without a greeting, dropped his eyes back to his comic book.

"Hello, Mr. McKay," Ralph said from the pier.

"Ralph!" McKay exclaimed. "How are you, son? Come aboard. How about a game of chess? I've been trying to work out a Banakin problem, but I must confess it has me stumped."

"I don't play chess," Ralph dropped lightly to the deck. "One of these days I'm going to learn, though."

"It's a wonderful game, Ralph," McKay said sincerely. Then, as if remembering something he suddenly snapped his fingers and chuckled deep in his throat. "You certainly took off in a hurry yesterday. Right after you left my mind started to function, and I sent Tarzan after you, but you'd already left the parking lot. It occurred to me that I could have called the hotel and got you relieved for the evening. But I was too late with the idea. And we could have used you, too."

"Oh, that's all right, Mr. McKay," Ralph said guiltily. A hard lump formed in his throat.

"I must apologize for my thoughtlessness, Ralph. And as I said we could have used you. You know something about diesels and our engines broke down right after we started back from Lauderdale." He chuckled richly. "Had to be towed back for repairs. I don't know what was wrong—Tarzan could probably tell you—but we didn't get back to the slip here till seven-thirty this morning. What was really funny—" McKay's eyes crinkled with amusement—"our *Sea Witch* sleeps six below, but because we had Maria aboard I had to let her have the cabin. Tarzan and I had to rough it out on deck all night!"

Ralph felt as though he had just been jabbed in the stomach with a hard right. His stomach quivered twice and then steadied.

"I sure am sorry, Mr. McKay," Ralph said hoarsely. "I wish I had been with you."

"No harm done," McKay said easily. "I'm only sorry I didn't think of calling the manager. Mr. Wallace owes me a few favors. Anyway, I think Maria had a good time. She's a nice kid, Ralph, and she certainly hates the idea of going back to New York. And I don't blame her. Personally, I think she's foolish to return. If she's a competent typist, and she says she is, I could find her a position down here. There are some people around Miami Beach who owe me a few favors, one lawyer in particular." He winked at Ralph. "But I think any business man would think I was doing him a favor if I found him a pretty typist like Maria, don't you?"

"Yes, sir."

"Maria evidently thinks a great deal of you, Ralph," McKay continued.

She did, Ralph thought. But not now.

"I'd like to do something for the girl. She isn't really tied down in New York. Her family can get along without her. I didn't tell her I could find her a job here. In fact, I thought it might be presumptuous and she might give my suggestion a mistaken interpretation. But if you care to, you might sound her out, and if she takes to the idea, let me know. Of course," McKay shrugged, "it doesn't make any difference to me one way or the other. Say! I think I've got Monsieur Banakin licked!" McKay closed the book of chess problems and faced Ralph with a guileless smile. "But a girl working for a lawyer, Ralph, has a chance to get some place. If Maria studies stenography at night school, and tries to learn something in the office, she can be a legal stenographer in a year or so."

"Yes, sir. I'll talk to her if you want me to, Mr. McKay."

"I don't want you to, Ralph," McKay explained quietly. "I thought *you* might want to. She's your girl, not mine. You like her, don't you?"

"That's an understatement, Mr. McKay. I don't know her very well, but I think she's one of the nicest girls I've met in a long time."

"Well, all right then! Would you like some coffee?"

"No, sir. I was going for a swim," Ralph lied, "and I passed by the Marina so I stopped to say hello."

"Glad you did. Give me a ring." McKay stood up and stretched.

Ralph said goodbye, waved an unacknowledged farewell to Tarzan and returned to his car. I have to believe him, Ralph thought. But I can't help wondering whether three free rides on his boat hasn't put me into one of the categories of Miami residents who owe him "a few favors."

The idea of going for a swim hadn't been a bad idea at that. Ralph ate a considerably delayed breakfast of ham and eggs at a roadside diner and drove to the employee's parking lot at the Rotunda Hotel. He changed into his trunks in the basement locker room, and made his way to the almost deserted two-hundred foot strip of sandy beach. At five in the afternoon, most of the hotel guests were taking advantage of the half-price cocktail hour in the Rotunda Room.

He stared into the blue-green ocean disconsolately. He would have to apologize to Maria. But how? Whether McKay was on the up and up or not, he would have to gain her forgiveness and somehow talk her into staying in Miami and taking the job in the lawyer's office. He knew that some way, any way, he had to keep Maria in Miami; he couldn't let her get away. His heart ached at the thought of never seeing her again. A slight smile played about the corners of his lips.

"You poor bastard," he said aloud with grisly humor, "you must be in love!"

SEVEN

AS soon as Maria entered the air-conditioned lobby of the Rotunda Hotel she stopped running and composed herself. With a piece of tissue she wiped the tears away from her eyes and, smiling bravely at the few guests sitting in the lobby reading the paper, she crossed to the elevators.

By the time Maria had reached the fourth floor and Room 419, she had dismissed the incident and Ralph's insulting remark almost completely from her mind. He didn't know anything. How could he know? He was sore because she had gone off in the boat with Mr. McKay to Fort Lauderdale. That was all. It had been a jolt, though—a remark like that out of the blue!

Maria inserted her key in the lock and tried to push open the door. The door was stopped by the chain lock and she had to waken Peggy.

"Peggy!" Maria said loudly. "Wake up. You've got me locked out!"

"Just a minute," Peggy called back. A moment later Peggy opened the door, and closed it behind Maria. Maria dropped her straw bag on the dresser, stretched out her arms and yawned happily. Peggy glared at her accusingly, her mouth sullen with resentment.

"Where have you been all night, Maria? I've been worried sick about you! Just sick!"

"Didn't Ralph tell you I went to Fort Lauderdale in the boat with Mr. McKay?" Maria lifted her eyebrows innocently.

"Yes," Peggy admitted. "He left a note in the mailbox at the desk. He telephoned it in. But I didn't find the note until after six, and by that time I'd made arrangements with Mrs. Barnes and that little brunette schoolteacher from Georgia. I didn't know when you'd be back, and we waited till the last minute and then we had to go. We had reservations."

"Did you have a good time?"

"Not really. I couldn't relax. I was so worried about you."

"I don't see why," Maria said wearily, beginning to undress. "You knew where I was."

"Not at eleven o'clock I didn't!" Peggy said accusingly. "You weren't back by then, and I didn't know what had happened to you. At midnight I walked down to the elevator and asked Ralph if he knew when you'd be back, but he just sort of growled at me. 'How the hell do I know, Madame!'" Peggy mimicked Ralph's angry voice, and Maria laughed gleefully, clapping her hands together.

"He was mad at me because I was supposed to be on a date with him and he couldn't go." Her eyes softened. "I suppose it was a dirty trick, Peg, but you would have done the same thing. We had dinner in Lauderdale with champagne and everything. I got a little high on the wine, I think, and went to sleep in the cabin around ten. At one A.M. Mr. McKay woke me. We were at the Marina in Lauderdale. They had engine trouble, and I slept through being towed and everything. But while they worked on the engines, Mr. McKay got a cab and we went to the Jamaica House. We had drinks and danced until three, and then his bodyguard telephoned that the boat was fixed and we came back. That's all, Peg."

"You could have called me."

"I didn't think about it, Peg," Maria said thoughtfully. "I was a little high and having a good time. I'm sorry."

"Well, all right. How about the Jungle Cruise? Are you coming along this morning or not?"

"No, I'm going to bed."

"We leave tomorrow," Peggy reminded, "and they say the Jungle Cruise is simply fabulous. You won't get another chance, you know."

"I'm just too tired. Don't forget I was on a cruise all day and all night."

"Do you want to go downstairs for breakfast with me? I have to leave with the tour at nine-fifteen."

"I had breakfast on the *Sea Witch*." Maria entered the bathroom and closed the door. She didn't want to be pumped any more by Peggy, not until she had all of the answers figured out first. Peggy could be relentless when she began to pick at details. Maria stepped into the shower, adjusted the nozzle to a lukewarm needle-spray and stayed under it until Peggy tapped on the door and opened it a crack.

"I'm going now, Maria. Sure you won't change your mind?"

"I'm just too tired, Peg! You can tell me all about it when you get back!"

As soon as the door clicked shut, Maria turned off the shower and toweled herself dry. She padded barefooted into the bedroom and called downstairs for a ten A.M. appointment at the hotel beauty parlor. A pleased smile turning up the corners of her lips, Maria sat down on the edge of the bed and slowly counted the crisp twenty-dollar bills three times. She enjoyed the rich feel of the crackling twenties. And there's more where this came from, she reflected. A lot more. And for what? Technically, I am still a virgin. She giggled. Not even technically, I *am* still a virgin!

In addition to the $260 given to her by McKay she had sixty dollars in traveller's checks, and three one-dollar bills in her purse. Tomorrow her vacation would be over, and she could return to New York with more money than she had when she left.

If she returned...

She had eaten breakfast with Mr. McKay in the cabin, crisp bacon and scrambled eggs from the galley, and both of them had acted as if nothing had happened. Mr. McKay certainly had looked the same, with a fresh shave and a soft white silk shirt. He had been so matter-of-fact about his outrageous proposition, just like a salesman talking to a prospective buyer at the Company.

"You're young, Maria," he had stated, taking a bite of scrambled egg, "and quite beautiful. To waste your life in office work is rather shameful, in my considered opinion. Within five years, if you care to put yourself in my hands, I can guarantee that you'll have enough money to retire. And during that five-year period you will live well, very well. Some of the things you'll have to do may be unpleasant to you at first—" at this point he looked steadily into her eyes, and shook his fork at her—"but you'll get used to it. Do you believe that?"

"Yes," Maria had blushed and looked down at the table. "I guess so."

"Any clerk you marry in New York," McKay continued, "with his measly take-home pay of a hundred a week will want the same things as the rich men I can introduce to you." McKay had paused. "The only difference will be the amount of money you'll have in the bank. If you want to stay here in Miami Beach I can guarantee you approximately $2,000 a month. At twenty, and with your face and figure, you'll make that much easily. Your virginity is worth one thousand dollars for your next job. A flat fee."

Maria had gasped. "A thousand dollars!"

"Isn't it enough?" McKay had said jokingly. "Most American girls give it away for nothing in the back seat of a car."

Maria had to leave the table. The frankness of McKay's proposition had embarrassed her, and she couldn't look at his face. For a long moment she had stared blankly at a color photo of a cream-colored yacht on a dark, blue sea.

"I just don't know, Mr. McKay," she had said at last, her back to the table. "I haven't been brought up that way. There *are* such things as morals," she protested mildly.

"You don't have to make up your mind this very minute. Think it over, but think practically. I'm not trying to push you into something you'll regret. If you really think you'd be happier living with some jerk in a Manhattan project apartment with two or three squalling brats at your heels—that's it. Sit down. Drink your coffee."

As Maria recalled the conversation between Mr. McKay and herself, she moved to the open window and watched the workmen as they scurried about their construction tasks on the site of the new hotel. Everything McKay had told her was reasonable, practical, and plain common sense. She had had similar thoughts herself, long before she had ever met McKay.

A young workman in the pit below looked up and saw Maria in the window. He removed his hard construction hat and waved to her, a broad smile on his dirty face. Maria laughed, and stepped back from the open window. No, she thought, nothing is for free, not even a look. Not anymore.

Maria dressed, and went directly to an exclusive women's shop next door to the hotel. Maria now bought a white satin bathing suit, paying the $30.00 without a murmur. She also bought a pair of straw slippers for $12.00, and an imported French silk scarf for $8.00.

She returned to her room, buried her new purchases beneath her old clothes in the bureau drawer, and then rode the elevator down to the beauty parlor, fifteen minutes ahead of time for her appointment. She submitted patiently to a shampoo and set, a manicure, a pedicure and a black-mud facial. Her bill was $25.00, and she handed the operator a five-dollar tip. The time was 1:15.

Maria went into the dining room and ordered luncheon: a rare sirloin steak with mushrooms, a baked potato, a chef's salad with Caesar dressing, and she topped off the heavy meal with strawberry shortcake smothered in whipped cream, and two cups of coffee. The bill was $7.50, and she left a two-dollar tip for the astounded waiter. As she entered the lobby, a gentle, refined belch escaped her lips. She put a hand to her mouth and glanced about her to see if anybody had noticed. No one had.

I've eaten too much, she thought. Eating like that every day, I'd get fat!

She crossed the lobby to the desk and made an appointment for the masseur to come to her room. She returned to her room, undressed, and rested quietly until the masseur, a putty-faced woman in her early forties, knocked on the door a few minutes later.

Meekly following gruff instructions, Maria was ordered into a scalding shower. The woman draped a thick rubber sheet over the bed. Allowed out again after five painful minutes, Maria's beet-red skin was rubbed briskly with rock salt by the masseur, and she was ordered back into the shower. Her tender body was roughly dried with a coarse towel, pummeled, kneaded, stretched and pounded again for forty terrible minutes before the relentless masseur finally stopped and covered her with a clean sheet. Too relaxed to move, Maria told the grateful woman to take fifteen dollars from her purse and to leave a call at the desk for four-thirty. She fell asleep before the door had closed.

Almost immediately, it seemed to Maria, the telephone rang and she was informed that the time was indeed four-thirty. Maria felt completely rejuvenated; every muscle in her young body was tingling and vibrantly alive.

Maria squirmed eagerly into her new bathing suit, admired herself briefly in the mirror, draped a terrycloth robe about her shoulders and rode down to the swimming pool. Three old ladies and two small children splashed in the shallow end; the old gray-haired lifeguard looked right past her. Maria disappointedly left the pool area and took the concrete path to the private beach. As she spread her robe to sit on it she noticed Ralph at the other end of the beach. He sat hunched over, clasping his knees, and staring at the sea.

Maria draped her robe over one arm and walked through the sand toward the wall and Ralph. Deep in his thoughts he didn't see her until her shadow fell across his face. Ralph looked up, startled, and when he recognized Maria his face flushed, and he tried to spring to his feet. Maria placed a hand on his shoulder and smiled radiantly.

"It's all right, Ralph," she said. "Don't get up." She shook out her robe, but Ralph quickly took it away from her, smoothed out the sand nervously and spread it for her. Maria sat down, put her arms behind her, and lifted her pale face to the blue sky. Her full breasts stretched the white satin of her new suit to the bursting point. Her eyes were closed and she breathed deeply of the fresh salt air.

"Maria," Ralph stammered, trying unsuccessfully to tear his eyes away from her straining breasts, "anything I could say would be inadequate. But I apologize from the bottom of my heart. I'm sorry! Nothing could make up for what I said. But I'm sorry. Sorry." He moved his hands in a helpless manner, and stared morosely at the sea.

"Never mind, Ralph," Maria said softly. "You were jealous and you wanted to hurt me. And for a few minutes you did. No one has ever talked like that to me before. But there was nothing between Mr. McKay and me, and you know it."

"I was a damned fool, that's all," Ralph admitted sorrowfully. "I didn't have any reason to be jealous, but that's all it was. We hardly know each other." Ralph nervously ran his fingers through his hair. "I don't know what came over me!" he said hopelessly.

Maria opened her dark eyes and inclined her head toward Ralph's troubled face. "Forget it, Ralph." She smiled her forgiveness. "I have. I've almost made up my mind to stay in Miami instead of going back to New York. And if I do, I'll want you for my friend..."

Ralph's stiffened facial muscles relaxed, and he looked gratefully at Maria. "Of course I'm your friend," he said eagerly. "You can count on me for anything. You don't know how happy I am you're going to stay in Miami!"

"Fine!" Maria laughed. They shook hands awkwardly and rather formally. "Maybe you can help me find a job!"

EIGHT

RALPH was not aware that Maria had no intention of finding a job. But he did immediately recall McKay's offer of a typist's job in a lawyer's office for the girl. He started to blurt out this information and just as suddenly changed his mind. Although Ralph did not normally have a suspicious nature, and usually liked almost every person he met, he was far from being dense. For two days his head had been filled with thoughts of Maria. Tommy Grant's sordid tale about McKay had been shrugged off as fantastic, but his mind had not entirely dismissed the story.

McKay had rather neatly disarmed him that morning by conveniently mentioning that he had remembered too late that he could have called the manager and gotten Ralph excused from work. Somehow, McKay's bland statement, coupled with an offer to find employment for Maria, and now Maria's sudden decision to stay in Miami, made Ralph hold his tongue. Admittedly, he didn't know Maria Dugan very well, but she had told him enough about her life to make him wonder about her hasty decision to stay in Miami Beach.

She was due to return tomorrow. Certainly her funds were low after a week at the hotel. Women didn't usually quit a good job until they had found a better one. Even a man holding a job he disliked intensely didn't quit until he could better his position; much less a woman. Maria's entire family was in New York, and so were all of her friends. Who did she know here? Ralph. A few vacationers like herself residing in the hotel. Tarzan and...Mr. McKay! Ralph lit two cigarettes and passed one of them to Maria.

"How about your friend, Miss Vittorni?" he asked casually. "Is she going to stay, too?"

"Oh, no," Maria laughed. "Peggy's an old stick-in-the-mud. She wouldn't leave the Company no matter what you paid her."

"Well," Ralph was still unwilling to mention the typing job, "I don't know if I can help you find a job or not, but I can talk to Mrs. Hirsch. She doesn't usually take in women boarders, but she likes me fairly well, and I think she'd accept you if I made a big pitch. The food is terrible, as I've already told you but her place is as cheap as you'll find till you start making money and find a better one. Without your roommate, if you stay here at the Rotunda, the minimum rate is fourteen bucks a day."

"You're sweet, Ralph." Maria patted his arm. "But you don't worry about me. I have plenty of savings so I'll stay on the hotel for awhile. If I don't find the type of job I'm looking for after two or three weeks I'll pack up and go home." She showed small even teeth. "My, you look glum! Aren't you glad I'm staying?"

"Sure I am!" Ralph forced an accompanying smile. "I was just thinking out loud. You know I'll help you any way I can."

Maria stubbed out her cigarette by burying it in the sand. "I believe I'll go in now. Peggy should be back pretty soon from the Jungle Cruise."

Ralph got to his feet, took Maria's hands and pulled her erect. They stood face to face, her breasts lightly brushing his chest. There was a friendly smile on her full lips, and her dark eyes were bold and mocking. On impulse Ralph put his arms around her, pulled her willing body in close against his own and kissed her. Maria's response was warm, but when he tried to force the tip of his tongue between her teeth she pulled away from him, shaking her curls and laughing.

"This is a private beach, I know," she laughed good-naturedly, "but not that private!"

"Don't go in yet," he pleaded. "Haven't you got time for a swim?"

"What?" Maria cried in mock dismay. "And get my thirty-dollar suit wet? No corrosive salt water will ever touch this suit!"

She snatched her robe up from the sand, turned and ran across the beach to the steps leading up to the pool area. Ralph watched the firm jiggle of her retreating hips with a pounding heart. At the top of the steps she turned, waved to him with a carefree gesture, and disappeared.

Ralph returned to the basement locker room. After dressing he sat dejectedly on the beach in front of his locker, smoking and thinking about Maria. He could not understand his attitude. In a sense he was overjoyed because the girl was staying and in another sense he was frightened. He tried to analyze the kiss on the beach. He was still thrilled by it; his nerves still tingled. What did the kiss and Maria's flippant remark hold for the future? Anything?

The warmth of her response probably meant nothing at all. To make something out of a friendly kiss was foolish. A beautiful girl is always getting kissed. He had kissed dozens of pretty girls in his time, and many of them had responded with hotter lips than Maria's. Just because he had fallen in love did he have to twist a simple kiss into meaning that Maria had fallen for him, as well? Wishful thinking, he concluded bitterly. Just because you're the only friend she has here…. Was he? What about McKay? McKay and his money? McKay-Money. Money-McKay! The two words meant the same thing!

With a curse Ralph slammed his fist into the unoffending door of his metal locker. With a cry of pain he did a mad devil's jig, circling the floor and blowing on his swelling hand. He rubbed his hurt knuckles gingerly, laughed angrily, and left the locker room for his car.

"You think too much, baby!" he addressed the pair of baby shoes dangling from the rearview mirror. "It's riding up and down in that cage every night for ten hours at a stretch. The narrow confines of that self-propelled, unpadded cell would make anybody crazy!"

There was still plenty of time to drive to Mrs. Hirsch's, eat dinner, and get back to work by eight. But not tonight. Another night in the claustrophobic atmosphere of that damned elevator would probably finish him off forever. He had to take the night off to blow away some steam. Get stinking drunk. Something!

He stopped at the first cocktail lounge he came to, parked, ordered a double shot of bourbon from the bartender on his way to the rear of the room, and went to the telephone booth. He called Johnny Townsend.

"Ralphie Boy," Johnny said delightedly. "How are you?"

"I'm fine. No, I'm not either. Johnny, will you do me a favor and take my shift tonight?"

Johnny laughed. "You should've called me earlier, Ralphie. I've got other plans for tonight."

"Well, who else could I get? I've been on for twenty-one nights straight, and tonight I'm going to get loaded."

"Let me think a sec, Ralphie."

Ralph waited, dug a cigarette out of the pack in his pocket and lighted it.

"Ralphie? You still there?"

"I'm still here."

"I'll tell you what, Ralph. They expect you to goof off once in a while. But if you called in sick, they'd tell you to come down and report to the hotel doctor. I know," Johnny chuckled, "I tried it once. But if you want me to, I'll call in for you and tell Old Sourball you're sunburned."

"Sunburned? I'd have never thought of that one!"

"It's a trade secret, Ralphie. But it always works. It makes 'em mad when you say you're sunburned, but this *is* Miami Beach, even if hotel employees aren't supposed to have any feelings. I'll call in for you and then Sourball won't catch you in a lie. He'll know it's a lie anyway, but they can't fire you for sunburn."

"I sure appreciate this, Johnny."

"That's okay." Johnny laughed. "You can lie for me some time. But you'd better show up tomorrow night, because sunburn is only good for one goof-off."

"I will. But the way I feel right now I'd quit rather than work tonight."

"One good thing," Johnny said cheerfully. "You'll feel worse in the morning! Have a good time, Ralphie."

"Thanks," Ralph said dryly. The line went dead. Ralph left the booth, tossed off his double-shot and ordered another, this time with a beer chaser.

The glow hit Ralph's insides after the second double. He sipped the cold bottle of beer, and realized he was hungry. His wristwatch reminded him that he could still make it home in time for dinner. Not that the meal would be any good, but he was paying for it whether he ate or not, and he didn't have any plans made yet for the free evening. Ralph bought a half-pint of bourbon from the package store next door, slipped the flat bottle into his hip pocket, and drove home.

Ralph was hungry enough for the natural diet dinner to taste good to him. He finished the meal, went upstairs to the community bathroom, filled a toothbrush glass with water, and returned to his room. He fixed himself a stiff drink.

What do I do now? he thought. It's been so long since I had a night off I don't know what to do with myself!

The thought of getting drunk all alone in his room was a dismal prospect, and yet he couldn't really afford to drink in bars.

That could cost a man a fortune. He switched on the lamp at the table which served as a writing desk, sat down, and looked at the three books he had brought with him. No, he didn't feel like reading. None of that heavy stuff, anyway. What about drawing something? He had sketchbook, pencils, water colors, and hadn't touched them once since the semester ended.

What he really wanted to do was call Maria, and ask for a date. Take her riding in his car, with the top down, the radio playing soft music, park somewhere, and...But he knew she wouldn't go tonight. Her roommate was leaving in the morning, and Maria would have to spend the last night with her friend. Maybe when Tommy came in at ten he could talk him into double-dating? Ten was still early in Miami Beach, and Maria would certainly go out with him if her roommate was included on a double date. That's what he would do. Humming to himself, Ralph fixed another short drink and waited until Tommy came home.

At a quarter after ten Tommy came into the room with a paper sack containing two steak sandwiches he had fixed in the Rotunda kitchen before signing out. He tossed the sack to Ralph as soon as he closed the door.

"I fixed these for you, Ralph." Tommy grinned. "The bell captain told me you were off with sunburn. What a lie! With your Florida tan you couldn't get sunburned if you stayed out naked on the beach all day."

"Thanks." Ralph unwrapped the wax paper and bit into a sandwich hungrily. "I had to take the night off, Tommy. Have a drink." He pointed to the half-empty bottle.

Tommy unscrewed the cap and took a long pull. "First one today! Let's kill this and get another. We haven't been out together at night for three weeks, at least."

"I was waiting for you, buddy boy," Ralph grinned, and dislodged a shred of meat from between his two front teeth with a fingernail. "Let's you and I double-date with Maria Dugan and Peggy Vittorni."

"If you let me date Maria I'll buy it," Tommy said. "Otherwise, no deal."

"That isn't what I had in mind. Maria has decided to stay in Miami Beach and find a job. Her roommate is leaving tomorrow and naturally she can't leave her alone on the last night. So I thought if you and I called and fixed up a double date, we—"

"No soap, Ralph. I only go for sure things, and that Peggy Vittorni isn't my type. Too much of a drag, man."

Ralph argued for several minutes, but Tommy was adamant in his refusal to date Peggy. He was good-natured about his objections, however, and said: "Remember, Ralph, I'm the Head Busboy. I've got my reputation to think of, so save your breath. Your trouble is hot pants. Not that I blame you, but why should I suffer? How long has it been since you've had a girl, Ralph?"

"About three months, maybe more. I don't know."

"Okay, then. I'll take care of you. Wait." Tommy left the room, went downstairs and telephoned, and was back in less than five minutes.

"Okay, Ralph," he grinned, "you're all set. I called Hazel and told her I was coming over with an unopened fifth of scotch. All you have to do now is take my place."

Ralph began to protest, but Tommy shut him up and issued instructions. After listening disinterestedly, Ralph finally agreed to go through with Tommy's simple plan.

"Okay, Tommy. I'll try it. Most of my night off is gone already. And I don't want to waste the rest of it."

"You won't, don't worry," Tommy told him earnestly. "Hazel may not be any great beauty, but she's a cinch."

A half hour later, Ralph was parked beneath a street lamp near an area consisting of Second World War "temporary" housing. There was a collection of wooden frame buildings badly in need of paint. Each wooden cabin was separated from the next by patches of weeds and assorted junk, and the gravel road between the double row of buildings was lighted by a single forty-watt bulb glowing dimly beneath the crudely lettered sign at the entrance.

As Ralph sat nervously in his car, trying to get up enough gall to look for Cabin Number Six, a woman's voice at the far end of the darkened gravel road drifted through the night. "Oh, but I'm sick. Oh, but I'm sick. Oh, but I'm sick." The voice repeated the four words monotonously, without hope of any aid, as though she were merely attempting to memorize the sentence. A man opened the screen door of the first cabin on the left and screamed angrily: "Why don't you die then!" He slammed the door shut and cursed. The hopeless feminine voice stopped for a full minute, and then started again, carrying through the humid darkness. "Oh, but I'm sick. Oh, but I'm sick…" Ralph removed the unopened fifth of scotch from its paper sack, scraped off the seal with his thumb nail, and tilted the bottle for a long pull. He screwed the cap on again, dropped the bottle into the paper sack, and grimly got out of his car.

Number Six was the third cabin on the right. Ralph's stomach felt like a ball of feathers was inside it expanding and contracting, but with a last shrug of his shoulders, and a sickly grin on his face, he tapped timidly on the door.

Hazel opened the door, and said gaily: "Come on in, honey! What took you so long?" She couldn't see Ralph's face in the darkness, but he opened the screen door and quickly stepped inside. Hazel blinked her eyes several times, and then said with a trace of sullen irritation in her voice. "Why, you ain't Tommy, honey."

Remembering Tommy's instructions, Ralph held out the bottle of scotch, and Hazel quickly took it away from him. As she removed the bottle from the paper sack a smile made her plain face lovely for an instant. The sullen look returned immediately and she examined Ralph with narrowed, suspicious eyes. "Who are you, honey?" she asked warily. "I'm expecting another fellow in a minute."

"I'm Tommy Grant's roommate," Ralph replied. "He told me he had a date with you, but the hotel called and he had to go back to work. Well, he didn't want to disappoint you after just calling you and all, so he asked me to take his place." Ralph smiled disarmingly. "But if you want me to go I will." Ralph reached out for the bottle of scotch, but Hazel stepped back with a short, dry laugh, clutching the bottle to her chest with both hands.

"Heh, heh, heh," she laughed nervously. "Why, I think that's mighty thoughtful of Tommy, honey. Why don't I fix us a little drink so we can get acquainted?" She opened the bottle and poured two large drinks into a pair of thick water glasses resting on top of the dresser. A half-empty pint bottle of gin was beside the glasses, and a cheap, green ten-cent store pitcher filled with water. "I ain't got no ice, honey," Hazel said without regret. "But there's water if you want it."

"A little water," Ralph said.

"What's your name, honey?" Hazel poured very little water into Ralph's glass and handed him his drink. As Ralph touched her hand he noticed that the woman's fingers were trembling.

"Ralph. Maybe Tommy told you about me?"

"Sure. Lots of times." Hazel tossed off her drink with a swift, backward tilt of her head, grimaced uglily, and poured another enormous portion into her glass. "Whew! Heh, heh, heh," she laughed dryly. "Scotch is sure smooth after gin!"

The room was small, containing a sagging double bed occupying half of the floor space, a dresser, and a rocking chair with a cane seat. An open door in the back wall revealed a toilet, a washbowl, and a crude wooden stand. On top of the stand was a two-burner hot plate. A pile of dirty dishes and a frying pan filled the washbowl. In addition to the large window next to the front door, there was a smaller window above the bed. On the narrow sill of the small window, Ralph saw a stick of melting margarine, a plate of sliced bread, and a jar of peanut butter. Hazel removed a stack of dirty clothes from the rocking chair and tossed the clothing on the floor next to the dresser. She indicated the chair with her free hand, and gulped from her glass at the same time. "Sit down, honey. Make yourself to home."

Ralph fought down an overpowering desire to bolt for the door. And then he sat down. Hazel began to pull open dresser drawers and slam them nervously shut again. After glancing in all the drawers, she began to paw through a black patent leather purse at the foot of the bed. Evidently, the telephone call from Tommy had caused Hazel to make a half-hearted attempt to fix herself up, but she hadn't met with much success. Her lipstick was on crooked, and her hair, hanging halfway down her back, was a dirty brown mane badly in need of brushing. Hazel obviously didn't have any foundation garments beneath her green, nylon dress, and as she leaned over impatiently to search her purse, Ralph was oddly excited by the bouncing motions of her large, low-hanging breasts beneath the thin material. Two bright spots of unevenly applied rouge on her cheeks contrasted sharply with her muddy complexion. Hazel had a fat round belly and wide thick hips, but her legs were long and well-shaped. She wore a pair of low-heeled white sandals on her bare feet, and her small, trim ankles were quite dirty. Ralph could not guess at her age. Hazel could have been twenty-five or thirty-five.

Hazel reloaded the large purse with the haphazard contents she had dumped on the bed, turned helplessly to Ralph with a crooked smile on her face and said, "Have you got a cigarette, honey? Heh, heh, heh. I had a whole carton someplace but I can't seem to find even a single pack."

"Sure." Ralph took two packs out of his trousers and handed one to Hazel. "Keep the pack, Hazel. I've got two."

Hazel put her drink on the floor, ripped open the package, and Ralph held his lighter to the cigarette in her mouth. She inhaled gratefully, removed a shred of tobacco from her tongue by licking the sleeve of her dress, and smiled coyly at Ralph.

"Tommy was lucky to catch me in when he called," Hazel said, winking at Ralph. "Heh, heh, heh," she laughed dryly. "I was just going to eat. I ain't had a thing all day. Are you hungry, honey?"

"Nope," Ralph said. "I just had two steak sandwiches." If she thinks I'm going to take her out to eat some place, she's crazy, he thought.

"Oh, I don't want to go out, honey! Heh, heh, heh. I thought I'd call down to the barbecue stand and send for some ribs. Do you like ribs, honey?" Hazel asked anxiously.

"Sure. Go ahead and call. I can always eat some ribs." And if I can't, Ralph thought, you should be able to eat two orders. Hazel drained her glass, picked up the telephone, and dialed what was evidently a familiar number.

"Deliver a double order of ribs, and a double order of french fries to Number Six, Garfield's Camp," Hazel said brightly into the mouthpiece. "Of course it's C.O.D.! I never failed you yet did I, Ed? And put on plenty of the hot sauce, not the medium. Fine. Sure, Ed." Hazel racked the receiver and placed the telephone on the floor again. She took Ralph's empty glass. "Looks like we're ready for another one. Heh, heh, heh," she laughed her dry, brittle laugh. "Honest to God, honey," Hazel shook her head as she measured out two drinks at the dresser, "people just don't trust anybody, anymore. I been buying ribs from Ed's Bar-B-Que for two years, and he asked me if I had the cash. I wouldn't even trade with a man like that if his ribs wasn't so good. I like the hot sauce. Sometimes, if you been drinking a lot, you don't get no taste to food unless you got a little hot sauce on it."

"That's right," Ralph agreed. Ralph knew that Hazel was having trouble carrying the conversation, but he didn't know how to take the lead away from her.

"I work at the Rotunda Hotel, too," Ralph said lamely. "The same place Tommy works."

"That's a nice hotel."

"Yes."

"This is a hard town to find a job."

Ralph nodded.

"It didn't used to be," Hazel continued. "Five years ago you could get a job anywhere. I'm a good waitress, but lately I just can't seem to get a job no matter how hard I try."

"It's tough, all right," Ralph sympathized.

For several minutes both of them were silent.

"How about another drink?" Hazel said suddenly. She startled Ralph, and he put a hand over his glass.

"No, thanks," he said. "I've still got plenty. You'd better take it easy too, Hazel. That stuff is powerful."

"Heh, heh, heh." Hazel's dry laugh was beginning to grate on Ralph's nerves. "I can drink scotch all night, honey. Don't worry about little Hazel." She padded to the dresser and poured another drink into her glass. Ralph was pleased to note that the drink was smaller than her previous drinks.

There was a rap on the door. "That must be the boy with the ribs. You get them for me, will you, honey? I got to powder my nose." Hazel went into the bathroom and closed the door.

Ralph opened the front door and accepted the brown-paper package from a small Negro boy. The bill was $3.50, and Ralph gave the boy four dollars, telling him to keep the change. Ralph latched the screen door, closed the inner door and shoved home the bolt. Six for scotch and four for ribs added up to ten bucks. No matter how he felt about Hazel, he intended to get his money's worth now.

Hazel came back to the room and took her plate to the bed. Ralph stood by the dresser to eat his portion, and watched Hazel strip the meat away from the bones. Her hands and face were soon smeared with sauce and, as she leaned over her plate, a wedge of brown hair fell over her eyes. Without wiping her fingers on her paper napkin she pushed the disheveled hair back into place with an impatient movement of her greasy, sauce-smeared right hand. Ralph shuddered, pushed his plate away and finished his drink.

"You can have mine, too, if you want," he said. "I can't eat anymore."

"Just leave 'em," Hazel said with a full mouth. "I've got plenty for now, but I'll eat 'em later."

Ralph went into the bathroom, washed his hands under the tap, and dried them with his paper napkin. There was a full, uncovered garbage can beneath the washbowl, and the odor of the garbage along with a strong smell of disinfectant made the bathroom a thoroughly unpleasant room.

Ralph went back to the other room, poured a double shot into his glass and drank it neat. Hazel scraped her remaining ribs and french fries on Ralph's almost full plate, and put the plate into the top dresser drawer.

"A little snack for later on," she explained, winking at Ralph. As she lifted her glass to her mouth she noticed that the door was bolted. The drink disappeared down her throat and she placed her empty glass on the dresser. She smiled lewdly at Ralph. Her face, mouth and chin were smeared messily with the red barbecue sauce. The food had helped some, but the rapidity of her drinking on any empty stomach had finally caught up with her. Hazel couldn't stand still without support. She lurched to the bed, steadied herself by holding on tight to the foot of the curving metal bedstead. She nodded witlessly several times, wiped her smeared mouth with the back of her free hand, and laughed meaninglessly.

"And now," Hazel said thickly, "I suppose you want a little action, huh?"

Ralph poured another drink, added water, and stared at the woman, his heart pounding heavily in his chest. Hazel hiked the green dress above her full hips, sat clumsily on the bed, and from the sitting position stripped the flimsy material over the top of her body and head. Her arms caught in the narrow sleeves, and when she whimpered deep in her throat, Ralph freed her arms, and draped the nylon dress over the back of the rocking chair. She fell limply back across the bed, and squirmed and hunched into the center of the sagging mattress to find the pillow with her head.

"What are you waiting for, honey?" she asked.

Under Hazel's amused and inviting eyes, Ralph began to take off his sport shirt. He staggered and almost fell. Hazel laughed.

"You're as drunk as I am," she said.

Ralph was a trifle dizzy but he smiled and shook his head. His mouth was dry with excitement as he looked down at Hazel's body. Hazel wiggled her fat hips enticingly and ran her tongue over her lips.

"Come on! What're you waiting for?"

Ralph grinned foolishly and held up one finger in reply. He went into the bathroom, took a sour-smelling towel from the rack, and wet the end under the tap in the washbowl. Hazel cheerfully submitted while Ralph wiped her greasy face and mouth with the damp towel, but when he sat down on the edge of the bed to critically examine the job, she jerked the towel out of his hands impatiently, and tossed it to one side. She grabbed both of his wrists, pulled him off balance and on the bed beside her. Ralph closed his eyes, sunk his hands deep into Hazel's thick dirty brown mane, and found her open mouth with his searching lips.

In less than an hour Ralph was standing beneath the shower in the upstairs bathroom at Mrs. Hirsch's Rooming House. Completely sober, sick to both heart and stomach, as the hot water sluiced over his head he repeated to himself: "I'll never be clean again. I'll never be clean again..."

NINE

THE argument between Maria and Peggy didn't begin until almost eleven o'clock, but once it began the two girls fought verbally until after three, and both were exhausted.

A minor argument ensued at six when Maria returned to their room from the beach and Peggy observed the new, thirty-dollar bathing suit. Peggy recognized the suit at once as the one both of them had been admiring in the window of the shop.

"Listen, Peg," Maria said wearily. "It was my money, I had it, and I bought the suit, so let's forget about it."

"But to pay thirty dollars for a suit when we're leaving tomorrow is crazy!" Peggy said. "You can't possibly wear it again until next summer, and suppose you put on five or ten pounds by next year? You won't be able to get into it!"

"I don't intend to put on five or ten pounds. And what I do with my money is my business, not yours."

The two girls went downstairs for dinner, and Peggy said nothing more about Maria's extravagance. The suit would have been a logical object to use to tell Peggy she was staying in Miami, but Maria wanted to put off telling her friend until the last minute. She knew that Peggy would have a thousand objections, and she didn't want to listen to them. Although her mind was definitely made up she was well aware of Peggy's persuasive powers, and she didn't want her mind to be changed.

Following dinner the girls sat in the lobby trying to think of something to do on their last evening.

"Well, Maria," Peggy said, smiling and shaking Maria by the shoulder. "We can't sit here in the old lobby all evening. It's our last night in Miami Beach so why don't we at least have a few drinks in the Rotunda Room?"

Maria agreed, and the girls entered the hotel cabaret and sat at their familiar table. They were soon joined by Mrs. Barnes, and a tiny hunchbacked girl from Atlanta named Alice. The three plain women depressed Maria. I am like an orchid, she thought, surrounded by three potted plants. But after tomorrow, I'll never come into the Rotunda Room again unless I have an escort—and he'd better be wearing evening clothes! Maria tried to brighten the party and, because she had plenty of money in her purse, paid the waiter for three rounds of drinks in a row, smiling and tipping him a dollar each time. Her generosity was making Peggy almost frantic with anger.

Mrs. Barnes and Alice departed for the ladies' room, and Peggy didn't have to hold her tongue any longer. "What's got into you, Maria?" she said angrily. "We're going to have to eat on the train tomorrow, you know! Let the other two pay."

"All right," Maria said amicably. "You can pay for the next round if you want. Oh, waiter! Four more Tom Collinses."

"I won't pay either," Peggy said indignantly. "Not until those other two have bought three rounds. We're together, and we'll split even like always."

"All right, Peggy," Maria agreed.

Mrs. Barnes and Alice returned to the table as the waiter arrived with the next round.

"Oh, another one already!" Mrs. Barnes exclaimed, seizing her beaded glass. "Gracious, we'll all get drunk if we don't look out!" The waiter, a weary, wrinkled man with aching feet, shifted impatiently from foot to foot as he waited for his money.

At this moment, Donald McKay, who had approached the table unobserved by Maria, took the waiter's upper arm and squeezed it. "It's all right," he said. "Put whatever these ladies are drinking tonight on my check. And add fifteen percent for yourself, of course."

"Yes, sir, Mr. McKay." The waiter bowed and returned to the service bar.

"Good evening, Mr. McKay," Maria said brightly. McKay wore a white Italian silk dinner jacket, and Maria was pleased by the reaction of her companions when she introduced him. McKay did not sit down and after the introductions were made he looked pointedly at Maria.

"Will you dance with me?"

Maria joined McKay without a word and they danced together on the almost deserted floor. McKay smiled and looked up into her eyes. With her high-heeled slippers Maria was more than a head taller than he was.

"Well?" he queried, raising his eyebrows.

"Yes," Maria said. The drinks were mild at the Rotunda, only one jigger of gin to a very tall glass, but three in a row had emboldened the girl. "I don't have to do any more typing to help me make up my mind. I've done enough typing already to last me the rest of my life."

"Good," McKay approved. "Call me tomorrow at noon."

"Call the *Sea Witch*?"

McKay laughed. No. Call the penthouse here at the hotel. I don't spend all of my time on the water. I only wish I could."

"I'll call at twelve, then."

"You're a wonderful dancer, my dear," McKay said, "but I find your height, in this type of embrace, a trifle disconcerting." He walked Maria back to the table, bade the group good night, and left the Rotunda Room.

The waiter, now aware that the more drinks he brought to the table the greater his eventual tip would be, paid close attention to their needs. But after the familiar floor show, Peggy insisted that it was time to go upstairs. Maria and Peggy said goodbye to Mrs. Barnes and Alice. The school teacher and the tiny woman from Atlanta had no intention of leaving as long as the waiter brought them free drinks.

On the way up to their room Maria asked the elevator operator, one of the night bellboys, where Ralph was tonight. The bellboy shrugged and said he didn't know. I wish he had called me, she thought, dreading the scene ahead. Peggy busily packed her suitcase, tidily and efficiently, and Maria sat in the chair by the window watching her sullenly.

"Aren't you going to pack, Maria?"

"No."

"I'll be finished in a minute. Lay out what you're going to wear on the train and I'll pack the rest for you. I don't mind packing; I'm only glad to be going home."

Maria lit a cigarette, stared thoughtfully at the glowing tip, and said sharply. "I'm not going with you, Peggy!"

For a moment the statement didn't register, and then Peggy stopped in the middle of folding a blouse and sat down on the edge of the bed. "I've known all evening something was the matter. Now, what is it?"

"I'm just not going, that's all. Period. You met Mr. McKay this evening. Well, he offered me a job here in Miami, and I'm taking it."

"Are you sure that's all he offered you?" Peggy said angrily.

"What do you mean by a crack like that?"

"All right, I'm sorry. But what do you know about him? What kind of a job is it?"

"It's a typing job. I'm sorry to spring it on you like this at the last minute, but this is a good opportunity. New York hasn't anything to offer me—"

"What about your mother?" Peggy broke in. "Your brothers and sisters? And what about Sidney? Don't any of those people mean anything to you?" Tears began to roll down Peggy's cheeks. "Don't I mean anything to you?"

"Don't cry, for goodness sakes!" Maria said anxiously. "I'm not committing a crime!"

"All right, Maria," Peggy said, wiping her eyes with the collar of the unfolded blouse. "I'll stay, too. If that's what you want. I'm a good typist; I know billing and office administration. I'll find a job here, too. Maybe we can get an apartment together somewhere, and—"

"But I don't want you to stay!" Maria shouted injudiciously.

Maria's cutting remark was the turning point. The disagreement turned into an argument after that, ending at three A.M. when Peggy had finally cried herself to sleep. Although Peggy had brought up every objection she could muster, Maria had stood firm. When Peggy had harped on and on about how badly her family would feel, Maria had cried for a few minutes, but she stopped abruptly when she realized that crying would make her eyes red, and probably swell both eyelids. A hurried visit to the bathroom mirror reassured her, and she returned to argue with renewed vigor. When Peggy had snuffled herself to sleep, Maria had a moment of delicious satisfaction before she closed her eyes. This is the best thing that ever happened to me, she reflected; when Peggy leaves tomorrow I'll be free for the first time in my life! A moment later she was asleep.

The next day, on the way to the railroad station, Peggy broke down momentarily. But she quickly recovered.

"Where will I write you, Maria?" she asked piteously. "I'm going to write every day. I want you to know that you have one friend left in the world."

"I know you're my best friend," Maria squeezed the troubled girl's hand. "I can't afford to stay at the hotel, but Ralph promised to find me a room in a good boarding house. So until I write and send you my address, just write to me General Delivery, Miami Beach."

This remark made Peggy laugh. "Do you know something, Maria? I think this is the first time I've ever admired you. I've always loved you, but mainly because you're beautiful, I think. For years I've made you do anything I wanted you to do. And now it turns out that you've got ten times as much will power as I have. The thought of staying down here alone in this strange city and taking a new job really terrifies me. But you act as though it's the most natural thing in the world."

"Well, isn't it?" Maria said seriously. "To get ahead in life is the American way."

In reply, Peggy kissed Maria on the cheek and pressed some bills into her hand. "I cashed in what was left of my traveller's checks. You may need some more money before you get paid, and I've plenty left to get home on. Here's your return ticket. It's only good for thirty days, you know. After that it costs extra. Promise me you won't cash it in until after you see what the job is like?"

"I promise." Maria put the bills and ticket into her purse and snapped the clasp. She didn't want to take Peggy's money, but to object would not only appear foolish; it might invite suspicion.

Maria did not wait on the platform to wave goodbye through the window. As soon as Peggy climbed aboard, she took a cab and went back to the hotel. When she paid the driver at the entrance to the Rotunda and turned around, the doorman was blocking her way. He tipped his cap and told her that the manager would like to see her in his office.

"What does he want to see me about?" Maria asked.

"He didn't say, Miss Dugan," the doorman said politely. "Do you know where his office is?"

"Next to the desk, isn't it?"

"No, ma'am. That's the assistant manager. Mr. Wallace is on the mezzanine." The doorman followed her inside, and pointed to the staircase. "The steps are quicker than waiting for the elevator."

"Thank you," Maria handed the doorman a quarter, and mounted the steps. She was bewildered. Her rent had been paid in advance, and wasn't due again until three that afternoon. What he probably wanted, she concluded, was to put another girl in with her to save her money. Well, he had another thing coming, because she was going to keep that room for herself!"

Maria opened the door marked MANAGER without knocking and entered. Mr. Wallace, a portly man in his early forties, got up from his desk and greeted her by name. "Good morning, Miss Dugan! I hope I haven't inconvenienced you by asking you to come to my office, but I wanted to handle the changeover personally."

"What changeover? I don't want to share my room with anyone else!"

Wallace laughed throatily. "Of course not," he said. "But I'm sure you'll like your new room." He turned to his secretary. "I'll be back in about five minutes, Grace." The manager held open the door for Maria, led the way to the elevators. Johnny Townsend was the operator on duty and he greeted Mr. Wallace respectfully.

"Nine, Johnny," the manager said sharply. "Express!"

"Yes, sir."

"Nine is the penthouse, isn't it?" Maria asked anxiously.

"No, Miss Dugan. Penthouse is Ten." Before Maria could phrase another question the elevator had stopped at the ninth floor.

The door to 901 was ajar, and the manager nodded for Maria to precede him. A maid was arranging a bowl of red roses on the coffee table in front of the divan, and Mr. Wallace jerked his thumb for her to leave. The maid closed the door as she tiptoed out.

"I believe you must have the wrong Miss Dugan," Maria shook her head disbelievingly. "I can't afford anything like this!"

The room was large, with a sliding glass door on the ocean side leading to a loggia wide and deep enough for two aluminum chairs and a small cigarette table. The furniture was modern, all in the same tint of eggshell, and the wall-to-wall carpeting was rust-colored. The walls and ceiling were pink, but the rusty shade of the carpet was picked up again by the floor-to-ceiling drapes bordering the glass sliding door. In addition to the red roses on the kidney-shaped coffee table, there was a bowl of yellow pansies on top of a V-shaped bar in the corner.

Mr. Wallace opened the door to the bathroom, smiled, closed it again, and then opened the sliding closet door beside the entrance. All of Maria's clothes were hanging on the rack. Maria crossed to the closet, pulled out the top built-in dresser drawer, and discovered the rest of her belongings neatly folded away.

"We took the liberty of moving your things, Miss Dugan. I'm certain everything is here."

"I'm not worried about my clothes. I know I can't afford this room, but if I could, where would I sleep?"

Wallace laughed, and pushed a hidden button below the padded armrest of the low divan against the wall. The back cushions rose silently, and a double bed made its appearance, quietly edging in the room to its full six-foot length on well-oiled wheels.

Maria clapped her hands together and giggled. "That certainly is clever! It makes this like a little apartment."

"We call it an efficiency, Miss Dugan. But there isn't any stove. However, there's a small refrigerator in the bathroom and an electric coffee-maker, in case you want to give snacks to your friends." Wallace turned away to show the bathroom again, and Maria blushed at the implication of what he meant by "friends."

"What is the rate for the apartment, Mr. Wallace?"

"Mr. McKay didn't say, Miss Dugan," the manager replied blandly. "And of course, whatever he decides is up to him. We usually charge two hundred and fifty a week in off-season, but I don't know what he has worked out for you. He directed the change and I made it." Wallace edged toward the door, opened it, and bowed. "Anything you need—" He pointed toward the white telephone on the end table by the divan. "Call me." He smiled professionally and closed the door, leaving Maria standing in the center of the room.

That will be, she thought with dazed realization, a thousand dollars a month! She blinked rapidly, turned slowly around, and took in the furnishings of the apartment with respectful admiration. In her head she divided thirty days into a thousand dollars and said aloud: "Thirty-three dollars a day, a fraction, and then the tax!" The daily rate staggered Maria and she laughed, shrugging her shoulders. "Well, if Mr. McKay is paying for it, why should I care?"

She walked to the bar and found full bottles of scotch, gin, and vermouth. Maria emptied a tray of ice cubes, and mixed a tall scotch and water. After turning on the radio, she sat down to nurse her drink and listen for the time. Promptly at twelve Maria lifted the white receiver and asked for Mr. McKay's penthouse suite. There was a short wait, and then the manager's voice was on the line.

"This is Mr. Wallace, Miss Dugan. When Mr. McKay isn't in his callas are always switched to me. He left word for you to go directly to his house. Do you know where it is?"

"No, I don't."

"Have you got a car, Miss Dugan? I mean a rental car?"

"I don't know how to drive. Not very well, that is," she amended.

"All right, then. I could get a car for you, but perhaps you'd best take a cab. Mr. McKay lives in the Everglades Estates. There are only three homes out there and you'll see a big archway clearly marked Everglades Estates when you get to it. Mr. McKay's house is the second house at the far end. The gravel road then goes on past his house but dribbles out to nothing in the woods, so you can't possibly get lost."

"I'll find it, Mr. Wallace. And thank you."

An hour later, Maria's cab pulled into the sweeping driveway in front of Mr. McKay's house.

The rambling, one-story concrete-brick-and-stucco home, in dazzling white, appeared magnificent in its setting of tall Southern pines. The wide front lawn was a mat of well-kept zoysia grass and resembled a soft green rug fresh from the cleaners. Maria paid the cab driver the meter fee of eight dollars, rewarded him with a one-dollar tip, and waited until he had circled the driveway and headed back down the gravel road before she climbed the tree steps to the front porch. Maria pushed the electric buzzer beside the door, waited, and when the door wasn't opened immediately, she timidly tapped twice with the brass knocker. The knocker was in the shape of a winged phallus, the type tourists often purchase in Pompeii, but Maria didn't notice this until after she had used it. Her face flushed with quick embarrassment, and when the Filipino houseboy opened the door she couldn't meet his questioning eyes.

"Mr. McKay is expecting me." She looked down at her feet. "Miss Dugan."

"Come in, please." The small, brown houseboy bowed and smiled friendlily, standing to one side to allow Maria to pass. He closed the door, bolted it, then fastened a chain bolt above that. "You are very early, Miss Dugan. The party is not till after nine."

"I was told to—"

"I'll tell Mr. McKay you are here. Please." He indicated a chair.

"If you want a drink, fix what you like." He smiled and pointed to a semi-circular bar to the left of a set of sliding glass doors. "You maybe want something special; I fix it for you later."

"I'll just wait, thanks." The smiling Filipino in his tan pongee jacket and black trousers disappeared down a long hallway and Maria sat down gingerly on the edge of a low upholstered chair. The size of the enormous room and the luxuriousness of its furnishings awed the girl. The room was fully sixty-by-sixty feet, with enough chairs and divans to seat comfortably thirty people. The walls were a pale turquoise, and the ceiling was a deep, primary blue. This color combination, combined with a thick wall-to-wall rug matching the ceiling, made the ten-feet walls seem higher than they actually were. Built into the ceiling were three baby spotlights, an amber, a blue, and a white. An original Kandinsky, in an ornate golden frame, was the only wall decoration. No attempt had been made to match the decorator colors of the furniture with the blue background, but all of the foam rubber furniture was low-backed and comfortable. There were several end and coffee tables in the room, each holding a white ashtray.

Maria got up and walked to the glass doors which looked out on the patio. There was a kidney-shaped swimming pool bordering the back of the uncovered patio, but it was empty. A dismantled diving board assembly was warped by the sun, and partially hidden under a stack of folding aluminum chairs. The thick piney woods began on the other side of the pool, and deep in the forest. Maria could discern the white blossoms of a late-blooming oleander. She thought the white blooms were quite beautiful, set off as they were by the dark, slanting blue shadows.

"Are you sure you won't have a drink?" McKay asked kindly.

Startled, Maria turned quickly around and laughed. "I guess so," she said. "I was admiring your view."

"Scotch and soda? Or do you want one of those horrible Tom Collinses?"

"Scotch and soda is fine."

McKay, wearing a pair of dark gray slacks and a white, short-sleeved sport shirt, went behind the bar. Maria joined him, and watched him mix the drinks.

"Here you are." McKay smiled, handing Maria a tinkling glass. He lifted his own in a toast. "To your virginity!"

"To what's left of it, you mean," Maria laughed easily, and they clinked their glasses gently together.

"And now, money talks." McKay tasted his drink, and then put it firmly down. He left the bar and crossed to the painting. He took a firm grip on the molding and whipped the frame open like a door. Maria remained standing and watched him work the combination of the wall safe that had been hidden by the picture. This is like a movie, she thought; I've never seen a safe like that except in movies.

McKay returned to the bar, opened a black metal box, and shuffled through a stack of gray-green traveller's checks. He counted them a second time, and handed the stack to Maria. "A thousand dollars," he said lightly, "in unsigned traveller's checks. They're perfectly good, Maria, and much safer than cash. There isn't any point in returning to the city and then driving out again this evening. So signing them on the top line will give you something to do this afternoon."

"I didn't know you could get unsigned traveller's checks from the bank," Maria said. "But I'd rather have them than cash."

"You can't," McKay said. "But I can. Go ahead and count them."

Maria pushed her glass to one side and slowly counted the checks as she placed them one by one on the bar in front of her. The checks were in twenty-dollar denominations, and when she had finished counting them, she looked quizzically at McKay.

"I must have made a mistake," she said hesitantly. "I only counted five hundred dollars...?"

"That's right," McKay explained patiently. "I gave you a two hundred and sixty dollar down payment on the *Sea Witch*. Your apartment at the Rotunda is two-fifty a week. But I discounted the ten dollars you had to pay for cab fare out here. And that's it. One thousand even."

"Yes, but—" Maria's face flamed with swift anger. "Who told you to move me into that expensive apartment in Miami for only one hundred, or one-fifty a month at most!"

"That's enough, Maria!" McKay said sharply, narrowing his eyes. "You don't *tell* me anything! Get it straight and get it through that little head of yours once and forever. *I* do the telling! From now on. You'll live where I tell you to live, and you'll do what I tell you to do! Do I make myself clear?"

The angry retort on the tip of her tongue was checked; there was a strong positive ring to McKay's voice that Maria had never heard before. With trembling fingers, she opened her purse and dropped the stack of traveller's checks inside. For the first time Maria realized that this was a serious business she had gotten herself into. This wasn't a child's game a person could quit when she got tired of playing. And she was too late to get out of it...

McKay placed a gentle hand on her shoulder and Maria could not control the perceptible shudder that ran down her back. "Now we don't want to fight, do we, Maria?" McKay's tone was kind and soothing, which frightened Maria even more than his angry voice. "I look after you girls like a father. When you have troubles, I take care of them. We're going to be friends, aren't we?"

"Yes, sir."

"That's the ticket." He smiled and nodded. "Now, bring your drink along and I'll show you to your room."

Maria picked up her glass and followed McKay across the deep carpet toward the hallway. A hard lump formed in her throat and she fought back tears with all of the strength she could muster. "You girls!" He might as well have said, "You whores!" That's what he meant, and whether you were paid two hundred dollars or two dollars, or twenty-five cents, the members of the world's oldest profession were all lumped together under the single ugly word.

Maria's room was the first one on the left of the hall. McKay opened the door, and politely allowed her to precede him. The room was an ordinary bedroom, containing a wide double bed, two occasional chairs, a small desk, and a door leading into a bathroom. The room was windowless. The extraordinary feature was the two large, square mirrors; one paralleling the bed, the other on the ceiling above the bed.

"There's a pen in the drawer," McKay said, pulling the chair out from the writing desk to seat Maria. "Your costume for tonight's party is in the closet, but don't touch it. I'll have someone help you dress later."

Maria opened the drawer, and took out a white ballpoint pen. She twisted in her chair to face McKay. "I'm sorry about my outburst, Mr. McKay," she said apologetically. "I'm nervous, very nervous about tonight."

"It's perfectly understandable. I'm not angry, my dear, not as long as we understand each other." McKay entered the bathroom, and reappeared a moment later with a glass of water, which he handed to Maria. In his other hand were three white pills. "Take these," he said kindly. "Two are aspirins and the tiny one is codeine. They'll help you relax."

Maria obediently swallowed the pills, and drank the entire glass of water. "What do I do now, Mr. McKay? Just sit in here for the rest of the afternoon?"

"That's right. Take it easy. Sign your checks, and then take a little nap. Later on I'll have the houseboy wake you and bring you a nice little steak. You can take a shower, and by that time one of the girls will be here to help you dress. All right?"

"Yes, sir. Thank you for the pills. I feel better already."

As soon as McKay had closed the door, Maria signed the top line of all the checks. The room was soundproof quiet except for the hissing streams of air coming from the air-conditioning ducts. After signing her checks, Maria removed her blouse, skirt and shoes, and lay down on the bed. She felt drowsy, and somehow contented. She thought back to the night on the *Sea Witch* and the childish sex play with Mr. McKay. If she hadn't been so tight she would probably have enjoyed it. What would tonight be like? For several years now she had wondered what it would be like to have a man make love to her. Well, tonight she would finally find out! There wasn't anything really wrong with it. People did it all the time. In the quiet room she could almost hear the excited thumping of her heart.

She could see the length of her full figure in the mirror on the ceiling; her dark head on the white pillow; the swelling thighs beneath the white slip, and the long tapering legs. She cupped her breasts with both hands, watching herself in the polished ceiling mirror. Her eyelids were getting heavy and she allowed them to close.

"Well," she said, yawning lazily, "whoever gets me tonight: you sure are a lucky man!"

TEN

RALPH awakened at ten A.M., and sat on the edge of the bed for fifteen minutes, smoking two cigarettes before he got wearily to his feet and shuffled to the dresser. His headache was mild, but every muscle in his body was sore and tired. He swallowed two dexedrine and three aspirin tablets without water, grimaced at the dry taste in his mouth, and sat on the edge of the bed again. The memory of Hazel crowded his mind with confused images. His remembered thoughts were worse than his scotch hangover.

The dexedrine lifted Ralph's depression enough for him to take yet another shower, and shave; and then he returned to his room and sprawled on the bed again. The square of sunlight across his bare legs, shining in from the window, brightened the shabby room. In his mind Ralph compared Maria to Hazel, point by point, inch by inch, but this mental torture only increased his self-disgust. I must have been crazy, he thought, to get mixed up with a woman like Hazel.

Lethargically, Ralph dressed, pulling a T-shirt over his bare chest and slipping into a pair of faded khaki shorts. He changed belt and money from the slacks he had worn the night before, shoved his feet into a pair of scuffed loafers, and went downstairs. At the door, Mrs. Hirsch called to him, and he turned to face her with his hand on the knob.

"Mr. Tone," she said. "Mr. Grant called and asked for you to wait for him. He wants to see you, he said. I didn't call you to the telephone because I thought you were still asleep."

"I was. Thanks." Ralph opened the door and stood for a moment on the front porch, blinking in the bright sunlight.

"You didn't have any breakfast," Mrs. Hirsch reminded him from inside the house, chirping through the screen door. "Would you like me to bring you a nice glass of carrot juice?"

"No, thanks," Ralph replied. "I'm going to take a walk. If Mr. Grant calls again, tell him I'll be back."

Ralph walked two blocks to Mom's Cafe, and ordered coffee and toast. He was unable to eat the toast, but after three cups of coffee, he began to feel human again, and his headache was gone.

The beach is the answer, he thought. A few hours in the sun, a few refreshing dips in the water, and I'll wash Hazel out of my mind. Then I can face Maria with a clear conscience, but if Tommy wants to see me, it's too much of a drag to make it to the beach and back again before two. Ralph returned to the rooming house, made two piles of dirty laundry, one of his roommate's and one of his own, wrapped each bundle in a dirty shirt and took them down to his car. He sat on the front steps soaking up sunlight, until the tinkling dinner bell sounded inside for lunch. Ralph didn't eat any of the boiled vegetables, but managed to swallow two glasses of beet juice and one of celery juice before he returned to his room. His body was damp from sitting in the hot sun so he took a long cold shower and dressed again. Tommy entered the room a few minutes after two.

Tommy's face was troubled and he didn't greet Ralph with his usual exuberance. He sat on a straight-backed chair and looked seriously at him for a long moment. His roommate's steady gaze made Ralph uncomfortable.

"What did you want to see me about, Tommy?"

"Nothing much."

"Something's on your mind, Tommy. Spill it."

"I'm your friend—right, Ralph?" Tommy asked, mysteriously. "We're fraternity brothers, right?"

"Of course you're my friend," Ralph replied.

"I don't want you to get sore, Ralph."

"I'm not sore. Why should I be?"

"Because that queen-sized New York beauty, that lovely Maria you're so stuck on isn't a damned bit better than Hazel."

For an instant Ralph looked at Tommy's serious face. A second later he was straddling Tommy's legs, his strong fingers digging into the smaller man's throat. "Take that back, damn you!"

Tommy's eyes were steady and he made no attempt to defend himself. Under Tommy's direct, indifferent eyes, Ralph dropped his hands and shook his head sorrowfully. "You shouldn't say things like that, Tommy," he mumbled. "I'm sorry, but when you kid a man about the girl he's in love with, don't act like you mean it." Ralph sat down on the edge of his bed, his chin on his chest.

Tommy rubbed his neck with the tips of his fingers. "I told you not to get sore, Ralph," he said. "But I am serious. Before I say anything else, go downstairs and call Maria Dugan at the hotel. Say you're Mr. Smith, and ask for Miss Dugan in 901."

"That isn't Maria's room. Nine is all apartments."

"That's right," Tommy agreed. "Two-fifty a week in summer, three-fifty a week during the season. Make the call."

Ralph hesitated, a fresh question ready, but Tommy jerked his thumb at the door. "Go ahead. Call. Find out."

A few minutes later Ralph came back and sat down. His eyes were puzzled as he looked at his friend. "I called, Tommy, but she wasn't in. Dugan is a common name; maybe she—"

"Wake up, Ralph!" Tommy said sharply. "I know where she is. She's out at Mr. McKay's Everglades Estate house! You know the two other high class call girls on the ninth floor. Miss Snootybutt, registered as Mrs. Green, and that other woman, Mrs. Mattox. Both of them are supposed to be grass widows, but we both know different, Ralph, so why kid yourself? They're both in the two hundred bucks a night class, and your sweet Maria has joined their ranks."

"How do you know so damned much?" Ralph said angrily. "You're just putting a lot of below-the-belt guesses together! Maria said she had a lot of savings. She might have moved to 901 for the view. Did you ever think of that?"

"No. And you don't think so either. Look, Ralph, I'm not a snooper, but there aren't any secrets from hotel employees. If you weren't my buddy I wouldn't say anything, but I don't want you taken in by any prostitute. You were drunk last night, sure, but you were talking too damned seriously about Maria to suit me. When you mentioned marriage, I thought I had to do something."

Both of them were silent for a full minute, and then Ralph cleared his throat. "Okay, Tommy," he said hoarsely. "I'll listen."

"First of all, I had a break. Bruno Fisk is back in town."

"Who's Bruno Fisk?"

"The waiter. The guy who first told me about the little parties out at Mr. McKay's house. He came into the locker room this morning, prosperous as hell. When he left for Palm Beach about three weeks ago, his new job didn't pan out, so he picked up with a rich gay boy on vacation. He shacked up with him and before his lover left for Cleveland he bought Bruno a second-hand Porsche as a going-away present. Bruno showed the car to us in the lot. It's some wheels, Ralph, gray, plenty of chrome. He needs a new top, but—"

"I don't care about the car, Tommy."

"All right. I'm just telling you the way it happened. While I was looking at the car, I tried to pump a little info out of Bruno. I lied to him. I told him I cleaned up three hundred bucks in a crap game, and that I'd like to spend it all at a stag party like Mr. McKay held.

"He gave me one of those real pitiful looks. Lit a big cigar, don't you know. 'It so happens,' he said, 'that Mr. McKay is having a party tonight, kid, but a measly three hundred bucks wouldn't get you into the kitchen as a dishwasher.'

"'I can get a little more,' I told him. Bruno laughed. He said my name wasn't big enough, even if I had enough dough, which I couldn't possibly have. I asked him how come he knew there was a party tonight, and he told me that he'd shown his new car to Tarzan down at the Marina, and Tarzan asked him if he wanted to tend bar tonight. He's loaded with dough now, and he said he laughed in Tarzan's face. This I doubt, because anybody who ever laughed in that guy's face wouldn't have been around to tell about it."

"Did you get anymore out of Bruno about what went on? Anything like that?" Ralph asked.

"No. I tried, but he clammed up. He got a little scared, I think. It's all right to put on the big shot act to the Head Busboy, but when we got onto McKay and the party, I could tell by his eyes that he was afraid he'd said too damned much. And when I left he grabbed my arm and made me promise to keep still about the party. 'Mr. McKay and his guests are too big for little people like us,' he said."

Ralph stood up and flexed his arms. "Where's Bruno now? I think I could knock a little information out of him, and I'd like to try," he said grimly.

"Halfway to Naples by now," Tommy said. "The guy from Cleveland gave him some addresses of some guys on the West Coast, and he was driving over to stretch his luck. I don't think we'll see Bruno in Miami Beach again. He was only driving through, and he just stopped to brag to us peasants."

"Okay. The hell with Bruno. What about Maria? How do you know she went out to McKay's house?"

Tommy grinned. "Big Tim, the doorman. After lunch I took him a turkey sandwich. And I loaded it with plenty of mayonnaise and sliced tomatoes. I smoked a cigarette while I waited for the plate, and I casually asked him if he had seen Miss Dugan. He's a pretty surly guy as a rule, but the free sandwich softened him up. 'Why?' he asked me. 'Nothing,' I said. 'Only Miss Dugan asked me to tell her when we had some fresh red snapper. And I called her on the house phone to tell her, and she wasn't in.' Then he told me she went out to Mr. McKay's home at Everglades Estates."

"You're quite a little detective, aren't you?" Ralph said bitterly.

"Aren't you glad to know? You don't think I enjoy snooping around and lying, do you?"

"I'm sorry," Ralph apologized. "But I don't know! I've got to find out for myself. How did you find out Maria moved to 901?"

"My keys," Tommy grinned. "As the Head Busboy I keep the keys to the orange juice and dairy refrigerator. And when the room waiter signed the order for cream and orange juice for Miss Dugan's apartment on the ninth floor, I asked him if it was the same Miss Dugan who had been on Four. He said yes, and when I had a little time I confirmed it with Jonny Townsend on the elevator."

Ralph nodded. "So far, Tommy, everything rings true like little bells. I don't doubt anything you told me, but I still don't know anything. You heard this and you heard that, and so on, but what it adds up to is Maria changing her room, and then being invited to a party at Mr. McKay's house. Do you see what I mean? I can't accuse her of a single thing unless I know definitely. McKay could be having an innocent party. I can't put trust in what a guy like Bruno says. He thinks it's an honor to be a male prostitute. With a mind like that he could say anything."

"You're a hard man to convince, Ralph," Tommy said, throwing up his hands with exasperation.

"I love her, that's why." Ralph buried his face in his hands, sobbed dryly, and then composed himself. He breathed deeply through his nose and looked down at the floor.

"Ralph," Tommy said softly, "don't let it get you, boy. I think I know how you feel about the girl, but facts are facts. Forget about her. Go to work tonight and get her off your mind. Maria isn't worth stewing about."

Ralph's brown eyes were dark and hard. His lips were tight. "I'm going out to McKay's house tonight. I'll find out."

"Be reasonable, Ralph. What about your job? You were off last night. If you don't show up tonight you'll be fired."

"So? I'll find another job. But if it's true I'm going home to Orlando, anyway. I couldn't stay here in the same place with her. But I know it isn't true. There's a logical explanation for all this circumstantial evidence, and I'm going to find out what it is!"

"Okay, if that's what you need to satisfy you. I'll take your shift tonight. I'll get a bellboy to ride the cage till I finish up, and then I'll take over."

"You don't have to do that, Tommy," Ralph protested.

"And you don't have to go back to Orlando either! No matter what you find out, be a man about it, Ralph. Do you know where McKay lives?"

"Yes, I think so. I've never been to his house, but I know where it is."

Tommy left his chair and crossed to the window. He leaned on the sill and looked down at the empty lot next to the house. "If I ever fall in love," he said sourly over his shoulder, "I hope it's with an old lady in her fifties, whose only concern in life is whether I'm warm enough at night and whether I've had enough for dinner." He looked down at the lot again. "And I hope I'm in my late sixties when the crazy thing hits me!"

The night was warm; the air was moist and sticky. Ralph stopped his car below the concrete archway announcing in faded red letters that the road to the right held the Everglades Estates. A few yards beyond the arch the moon's dead light reflected in a wide puddle of muddy water. The fresh, clean gravel of the road leading into the Estates resembled gold in the moonlight. Several hundred yards down the gravel road, he could see a pale porch light shining through the pines on the first house in the Estates. It wasn't possible to back his car into the woods because of the ditches on both sides of the country road, and yet he was apprehensive about driving into the Estates. However, there was little choice; he couldn't leave his car parked without lights on the narrow country road; someone would crash into it. Ralph got back into his car and turned into the gravel road. In first gear, and with the engine barely idling, the twin straight pipes of the exhaust still growled noisily. He passed the old woman's house, continued down the road, and pulled into the curving driveway in front of the vacant house. After stopping in front of the doorway, he put the gear in reverse and backed expertly into the empty carport and cut the engine. From here he would walk.

Ralph looked at his wristwatch. 8:30. Bending down, Ralph stuffed the cuffs of his trousers inside his socks as a precaution against stickers and sand spurs, and started through the piney woods bordering the gravel road. The moonlight helped him to see, even in the dark woods, and he picked his way through the uncleared brush. When he reached the edge of McKay's driveway he halted. A yellow light cast a golden glow over the white concrete porch, but there were no other lights to be seen. Two Lincoln Continentals, a black Cadillac sedan, and McKay's yellow Cadillac convertible were parked in front of the house, one car behind the other. The nose of a white Jaguar was poking out of the carport. The sight of the expensive cars disheartened Ralph. There was some kind of a party going on inside; Bruno hadn't lied to Tommy about that. And from the looks of the automobiles, if the guests weren't all big shots, they at least had plenty of money.

Staying well back in the woods, Ralph made a wide circle to the back of the house and squatted on his heels at the edge of the woods. The empty swimming pool yawned darkly, and moonlight reflected on the sliding glass doors opening onto the patio. Drapes covered the doors from the inside, and from the rear, the house looked as deserted as the house where Ralph had parked his car.

A light was turned on over a rear door to the left of the patio. Ralph dropped to his stomach, and from a prone position, watched the door fly open. A Filipino in a white mess jacket came out. He was carrying a round dishpan in both hands. He set the dishpan down, lifted the lid of the nearest garbage can, and performed a tricky dance step with shiny patent leather feet. He sang:

"Are you from Dixie?

"Yes, I'm from Dixie!

"Tra la la la la, la la!"

The Filipino stopped dancing, put a hand over his mouth, and giggled. Shrugging, he picked up the dishpan and began to scrape garbage into the open can.

Ralph wondered if he could bribe the Filipino into letting him inside the house. The little man was obviously a servant. Ralph whistled, two sharp notes. The Filipino turned his head toward the woods. His eyes were round, and Ralph could see the whites of his eyes under the glaring light shining above the door.

"Hey, buddy," Ralph called softly. "How'd you like to make a fast twenty bucks?"

The dishpan clattered to the ground; the Filipino scurried inside, closed the door, and the light went out. His movements had been so swift the dishpan was still rattling, and Ralph was blinking in sudden darkness. Cursing under his breath, Ralph retreated into the woods for a hundred yards before he stopped and pressed his back against a tree. That had been an unwise move, Ralph reflected ruefully. I should have got between the Filipino and the door some way, and then bribed him. The little bastard had been as quick as a ferret! Scared hell out of him by calling out that way. Ralph didn't believe the Filipino would say anything to Mr. McKay, however, and he didn't think anybody would search for a stranger in the woods at night. His car should be fairly safe, too. No one could see it unless they walked up the driveway to the empty house.

But what could he do now? He hadn't driven out here with any deliberate plan. He had thought of looking through the windows like a Peeping Tom to see what he could see. But there were no windows in that house! This picture of himself sneaking around now angered Ralph. Why not try boldness? Surprise them, the way they did it in the Army? Bang on the front door, and when it opened, rush on in. This idea frightened him, but it was the only way he could find out anything, and that is what he came out here to do—find out! With sudden resolution, Ralph walked through the woods, crossed the patio, and followed a narrow concrete walk which led him around to the front of the house.

His feet crunched on the gravel driveway, and he stepped into the circle of amber light. His feet wanted to run, but he made them climb the three steps to the porch. Under the yellow glow of the strong bulb, the red door had turned to pale tangerine. Ralph had been holding his breath without being aware of it. He now expelled his breath, and sucked several audible gasps of air into his lungs to free the tightness in his chest. Ignoring both knocker and door buzzer, Ralph tightened his fist and raised his arm shoulder high to rap on the door.

A searing white light flashed inside his head, his knees buckled and, as he fell forward, the fingernails of his lifeless hand made a faint scratching noise as they raked the wooden door.

ELEVEN

"MISS Dugan? Miss Dugan? You wake up now, please?" The voice was musical. A thumb and four fingers lightly gripped Maria's hip, and rolled her body gently back and forth. Maria was sleeping on her right side, both palms together and beneath her head. The pleasant voice was insistent, and Maria reluctantly opened her eyes. The hand lifted, and she looked up into the smiling face of the Filipino houseboy, Sanchez.

"You awake now, please?"

"Yes. But I sure was asleep!" Maria yawned and sat up, placing her feet close together on the floor. The houseboy lifted a napkin from a tray on the writing table. Although Maria was aware she was wearing a thin, transparent slip, she didn't attempt to cover herself in false modesty because of the Filipino. "What have you got for me," she asked. "Something good?"

"Steak!" He smiled. "Medium rare, no fat, no bone." He sliced the air with a stiff hand. "One half Irish potato. I take out of skin, mash, mix in parsley, butter, and stuff back in. Very good. Pot of coffee, three full cups. All right?"

"It sounds heavenly!" Maria went into the bathroom and closed the door. When she reentered the bedroom, the houseboy had gone. She dropped her skirt over her head, fastened it at the side, and put on her blouse before she sat down at the desk. She ate hungrily, cutting the tender red meat into large bites, and dipping each forkful into the fluffy potato before putting the morsel into her mouth. Maria had finished the steak and was drinking her second cup of coffee when the door opened and a young woman came in. The woman was very blonde with a pretty face and thick lips. She smiled at Maria, showing large white teeth. Maria thought the blonde looked like last year's Miss America, a winning entry from one of the far western states.

"The condemned girl ate a hearty supper," the blonde stated in a matter-of-fact voice.

"I was pretty hungry." Maria unconsciously put fingers to her disheveled hair. "I didn't have any lunch."

"Don't mind me, honey. My name is Helen, and I'm in this

show tonight myself." Helen wore a low-necked white peasant blouse, and tight red toreador trousers, tied with wide red ribbons below her knees. She had an alligator overnighter in her hands, and she dropped it on the foot of the bed. As she unsnapped the brass clasps, Maria smiled nervously.

"My name is Maria, and there's another cup of coffee if you'd like to have it?"

"No thanks, honey." Helen opened the suitcase and withdrew a rubber apparatus with four white elastic straps. She tossed it to one side and reached into the suitcase for a black satin slip.

"Oh!" Maria exclaimed, clapping a hand over her mouth, staring wide-eyed at the rubber apparatus. Helen quickly covered the piece of equipment with the black slip, and frowned.

"I'm sorry, Maria," she said, "I guess you've never seen anything like that before. Well, it won't hurt you. Temple and I use it in our act. I forgot you were the star of the show, I guess. I didn't forget, but I wasn't thinking. You look a little pale. Why don't you finish the rest of the coffee?"

"Oh, I'm all right," Maria said, tossing her curls. But she sat down again. "Who is Temple?"

"She's my partner. She'll be along pretty soon, and you'll get to meet her."

"How do you use something like that?" Maria asked hesitantly, blushing and gesturing feebly with her hand.

"Look, honey," Helen said kindly, "I'd rather not talk about it. Okay?" The blonde took a cigarette out of her purse, lit it with a gold lighter, and sat on the edge of the bed facing Maria. "You've probably got enough on your mind as it is. How do you feel, honey? A lot of big-winged butterflies in your tummy?"

"I've tried to keep my mind blank. I had a nap, and then ate the steak, but all I feel is kind of numb. It's not knowing what's going to happen that frightens me." Maria found it easy to confide in this beautiful girl.

"That louse hasn't told you a thing, has he?"

"You mean Mr. McKay?"

"Yes. Mr. Fifty-percent himself."

"Not yet."

Helen took a jeweled pillbox out of purse, opened it, and handed Maria a long yellow capsule. She went into the bathroom and filled a glass with water. Maria looked dubiously at the capsule in her open palm. Helen took two of the capsules out of the pillbox, swallowed them, and sipped from the glass.

"They won't hurt you, Maria. I always take two, but one should be enough when you aren't used to them." She handed the glass to Maria. Maria washed the pill down with the remaining water.

"What is it?" Maria asked, now that the pill was gone.

"It's a sort of king-sized tranquilizer. It works a little differently on each person, so I only gave you one. You don't get kicks or high on it like too much benzedrine, but your nerves quiet down. You know what's going on, but somehow you don't give much of a damn. But watch your drinking. When we meet the guests, just take one drink, and nurse it until the formal part is over."

"What is the 'formal part'?"

"I can tell you that much, but if McKay asks you, don't say I told you anything. Okay? This is a very screwy set-up McKay runs, but it's effective, and as long as the pattern works, I suppose he'll keep it. The men who come to these parties have really got the money, and they come because they aren't so young any more, and they need some pretty strong kicks. I'm not trying to frighten you, honey."

Maria tried to pour some coffee, but the liquid missed the cup and splashed into the saucer. She put the pot down, fumbled a cigarette out of her package and lit it.

"No, tell me," Maria said calmly. "I'm all right, and I want to know."

"Okay. Just take it easy. Sanchez said there'd be six guests to-night, so that means six girls, seven counting you. But you're the star, so you miss out tonight on the after-the-show revelries. Good word for it. Revelries. A word I learned at teacher's college.

"Anyway, Maria, during the formal part, the introductions, you'd think this party was an embassy gathering. We girls wear evening dresses; all the guests are in black tie and white dinner jackets. The guests like to think we're society girls or something. They know we aren't, but the way McKay introduces us, and the way we talk and all—well, you'll see. McKay sees to that. He circulates, and your partner doesn't even try to hold your hand. It's crazy, I know, when you think about what follows, but that's the way it is. Last time, I spent a half-hour talking to a New York

publisher about James Joyce, for heaven's sake! But then McKay
gives the signal and we pull out of the arena to our rooms.

"Sanchez shows movies while we get ready. By the way, it won't
hurt anything to give Sanchez twenty bucks, honey. He's a sweet
kid."

"Why? You mean as a tip?"

"Sure. He'll do anything for you, and he's kind. When a man is
kind to you without wanting something in this lousy racket, you
don't mind giving him a few bucks. And on top of that, Sanchez
treats you with genuine respect, not the spurious kind McKay
hands out."

"And the movies?"

"You won't see them. They're mild, anyway. Mostly for laughs.
After the movies, the girls each go back in and do their acts in
the center. Temple and I do a double, but all the other girls have
a single."

"You mean they sing or dance?"

"Well—I won't go into details. But there's an ex-director from
Broadway, a drunk now, and McKay has him dream up these
pantomimes and teach them to the girls. Still, it always costs you.
Temple and I had to pay McKay five hundred apiece for our little
act, and it lasts less than fifteen minutes."

"Gee, Helen, I don't think I could do anything like that. In
school it used to scare me to get up in front of the class to give a
book report!"

"Those pills will help. You'll get over being nervous. The di-
rector will probably see you later on this week. Don't be afraid
of him, and do what he tells you. He's a drunk, and liquor's his
weakness, not women. Let's see..." Helen thought for a moment.
"I guess that's it, baby. You sure are beautiful! How much did
McKay pay you? You don't have to tell me..."

"A thousand dollars."

"Is that all? Helen angrily ground her cigarette out in the white
ashtray on the bedside table. "Boy, he really takes his off the
top!"

"But it is a lot of money, isn't it?" Maria said, sorry that she
hadn't named a higher figure.

"Sure it is, honey. We all make it, but we sure as hell earn it.
I'm not saying anything against McKay, but we're supposed to

get fifty percent, and I know damned well we don't even get ten percent, much less fifty. But my bank account is growing all the time. For tonight, I get three hundred in all, one hundred for the entertainment, and two for the night with the guest. But McKay takes half, so that leaves me with one-fifty. Only none of us really knows what the guests pay, you see. We take what McKay gives us, and that's it."

"Couldn't you ask your guest?"

"Let me tell you something straight, Maria. Don't ask any questions, do you understand? Smile. Be nice, and do everything you're told to do, and you'll live to be healthy and maybe wealthy. Any tip your guest gives you, fifty, a hundred, whatever it happens to be, split it with McKay. Don't hold out."

"But you didn't tell me what I do tonight, Helen. What do I—?"

"I've told you enough already, Maria. You'll be all right. How about the pill? Do you still feel nervous?"

"I don't feel anything, Helen." Maria got up and made a small circle of the room and dropped back into her chair. "I'm not dizzy or anything."

"Try pouring the coffee again."

Maria picked up the silver pot with a steady hand and easily poured the remaining coffee into the cup. She tested the coffee with a forefinger. "Too cold to drink now, Helen. Should I open the door and holler for more?"

"You don't need any more, Maria." Helen laughed. "Remember, just take one drink. Now, let's get you fixed up. Did you take a shower?"

"I don't need one. I took a bath this afternoon before I came out."

"Okay. There's all kinds of make-up in the bathroom."

"All I ever use is lipstick."

"Put some on then, and afterward I'll dust some light powder on your face to accentuate your paleness. The paler you are the better it'll look anyway."

Maria went into the bathroom to paint her mouth, and Helen took down a long cardboard box from the closet shelf. She had it opened when Maria returned. "Take off everything, Maria," she directed. Maria removed skirt, blouse and slip, draped them on a wire hanger and hung them in the closet. "Bra and panties, too, sweetheart," Helen ordered. Maria unfastened her brassiere, dropped it on the desk chair and pushed down the panties over her swelling hips. With her toes, Maria picked the nylon panties from the floor, pivoted on the ball of her other foot, and kicked the wad on the bed. She lowered her long straight legs, took two swift steps to the middle of the room, and faced Helen with lifted chin.

"You feel pretty good, don't you?" Helen laughed.

"Not really, Helen," Maria giggled. "I used to do that trick with my panties when I was in high school. I just felt like doing it now, and I did. Am I supposed to feel giddy, or something? I feel fine."

"No. Just a little uninhibited."

Instead of using another brassiere, Helen covered Maria's breasts loosely with a black silk strip which fastened in back with two snaps. She fastened a wider strip of matching material around Maria's narrow waist, tucking it in at the back like a sash until the silk was smooth and tight over her hips. The lower edge of the shiny cloth fell halfway to Maria's knees.

"If that's too tight, say so," Helen said.

"I can breathe all right."

"Slip into this, then."

Maria leaned over with arms outstretched and Helen guided a long-sleeved net dress over her head. Maria stood erect and Helen gently tugged the flimsy netting down over her hips. The sleeves billowed out from the shoulders to the wrists where they were fastened by a single wrist snap. The white netting hung straight to the floor but after Helen gathered in the material at the back and tied a narrow red ribbon tightly around Maria's waist, the girl's full figure was clearly revealed through the open netting.

"Walk around the room and let me take a look at you, honey."

On her toes, Maria made three full circles of the room. The whiteness of her skin beneath the netting was emphasized by the two strips of solid black silk.

"This material is just like wearing air!" Maria said happily.

"Be careful. That outfit is deliberately designed to tear easily. There're gold slippers here to wear with it." Helen took the shoes out of the box.

"I'd rather wear my white ones."

"It doesn't make any difference to me, kid."

As Maria sat down to pull on her white shoes, there were two raps on the door, and Temple entered.

"You through already, Helen?" Temple said. "I was going to help you."

"It only took a minute," Helen said. "This is Maria, Temple. Isn't she pretty?"

"Lovely. The bride of Frankenstein."

"Cut it out, Temple!" Helen said sharply.

"I was only kidding. You look sweet, Maria." Temple bent down and kissed the girl on the cheek. The delicate scent of Chanel No. 5 filled the room. Temple was tall, with high cheek bones, and straight, blue-black hair. Her evenly tanned skin matched the shade of a highly polished olive. She was comfortably dressed in tight, black dungarees and a homemade blouse fashioned from cheap red bandanas.

"We've got Four and Six tonight, Helen, the rooms with the connecting doors. I put my suitcase in Four, so Six is yours, not that it makes any difference. Wait till about two A.M., knock and tell me you know a little game that four can play. By that time, I'll—"

"Later, Temple," Helen broke in, shaking her head. Maria isn't interested in our business."

"Don't mind me, Maria." Temple winked. "To me, business is business. We've got time for a drink before we glamorize ourselves, Helen. I'll get us a couple and meet you down in Four."

"All right. I'll only be a minute," Helen replied. "I want to brush Maria's hair."

"Do you want anything, Maria?" Temple said from the door.

"I'd better not. Thanks."

Helen brushed Maria's hair for a few moments, looked at the girl critically, and put her brush back in her suitcase.

Let's forget the white powder, Maria," Helen said. "You won't need it."

"Your partner, Temple, certainly is a beautiful girl," Maria said.

"That's true enough, and on top of that she's half Indian and half wildcat. Look, honey, I have to go. Will you be all right?"

"Sure. And thanks loads, Helen."

"I'll see you out in the arena in a few minutes. Just let that blank mind of yours stay blank."

"That's easy for me—I'm pretty dumb anyway."

"That goes for all of us, sweetie." Helen repacked her personal belongings, locked the suitcase and left the room.

Maria ran the tip of her tongue over her lips and held on tight to McKay's wrist when he escorted her into the living room. Resplendent in his midnight blue tuxedo, McKay had looked at Maria admiringly before leading her into the hallway, and had made flattering remarks to the girl to put her at ease. The candles placed strategically on low coffee tables filled the big room with dark, dancing shadows. As McKay introduced Maria to each guest in turn, she was unable to get a good look at their features. Five of the gentlemen, each introduced as "Mr. Smith," mumbled something politely and stepped back after Maria's timid acknowledgment. Temple, who was paired with the third Mr. Smith, squeezed Maria's arm gently but didn't say anything. The last guest, a shorter and fatter version of the others, had been talking to Helen, and clumsily kissed Maria's moist hand.

"This is General Smith, my dear," McKay said smoothly. "General, this is our little Maria."

"I'm going to buy you a drink, little girl," the general said. "Come on, Helen, let's go over to the bar, if we can find our way through this gloom without breaking our necks!"

Helen linked her arm with General Smith's, and McKay and Maria followed them. Maria accepted a tall scotch and soda from Sanchez; the general and Helen had the same. McKay wasn't drinking.

"All right, young lady," General Smith said sternly, looking into Maria's face with keen blue eyes. "I want you to tell me why a young maiden like yourself, evidently from a good family—"

"That's enough, General!" McKay's voice was sharp and decisive, but didn't carry beyond the bar area. He stepped between Maria and the elderly man, took the glass out of the general's hand. "Unless you behave like an officer and a gentleman," McKay stated in a low, unruffled voice, "I will have to ask you to leave. Your fee will be refunded, of course, and I'll see that you're on the next plane for Washington."

"All I was doing—" the general blustered.

"Was upsetting our little Maria," McKay finished the sentence. "I broke one of my rules tonight by allowing you to use the title you set so much store on, instead of a plain, anonymous 'Mister,' but I won't allow any abuse of these lovely ladies in my home."

There was a moment of silence, and then the general exploded with a snort of phlegm laughter. "All right, sir," he said. "I humbly apologize. Now may I have back my drink?"

"You may, sir." McKay returned the general's glass.

"Come on, General," Helen said diplomatically, "let's go back and sit down. I want to hear more about Manila."

"Certainly, my dear." General Smith bowed politely to Maria. "A pleasure to meet you, miss!" he said, "and I look forward to seeing you again—soon!" With another snorting explosion of laughter, he allowed Helen to lead him away from the bar.

"Cut him off," McKay said quietly to Sanchez. He returned Maria to her room. Maria had held onto her glass, and after McKay closed the door, she whirled around and held the drink up to the light.

"May I keep my glass, too?" she said, her dark eyes round with excitement.

"You may," McKay laughed. "We get all kinds sometimes, Maria. For the next couple of hours he'll think it's a long time between drinks."

"Now what do I do?" Maria asked.

"You wait. I'll come for you personally."

"And then what!" Maria said angrily, stamping her foot.

"That depends on you," McKay parried smoothly. "You can't say you weren't paid...and while you're waiting I'll lock the door from the outside. We don't want anybody mistaking this room for the men's room, do we?" And McKay was out before Maria could say anything else. His key scraped in the lock, and the room was silent. With a feeling of complete frustration, Maria threw her glass at the wall. It shattered into fragments. I should have finished my drink first, she thought. She sighed, shrugged her shoulders, entered the bathroom, and studied her face in the brilliantly lighted mirror.

The key turned in the lock and Maria rushed across the room

to meet McKay at the door. "How do I look?" she greeted him anxiously.

"Very beautiful," McKay automatically said. "Now we'll wait at the end of the hallway, and as soon as the fanfare stops, I'll take you under the light. Just stand there, do you understand? Nothing else."

"Yes, sir. And Mr. McKay, you will be gentle, won't you, and not hurt me or anything?" Maria pleaded.

"I wouldn't hurt you for the world, my dear." McKay patted her arm. "Come on, let's go."

At the end of the hall, McKay picked up the only candle still burning, and puffed it out. The soft background music stopped abruptly. The entire room was pitch black and, in the soft darkness, a man coughed nervously. A moment later came scratching noise, followed by a fanfare of trumpets. The amber spot in the center of the ceiling came on, flooding a soft square of fleece directly beneath it. There was another scratching sound after the trumpets stopped, and then the low sound of drumming began to fill the room from the hidden speakers. The drums were timed to the heartbeat, but Maria's heart raced ahead, and she stumbled as Mr. McKay led her into the circle of amber light. He dropped her arm and faded back into the darkness as the spot turned blue.

Maria wet her lips and looked shyly about her, but except for the faint outlines of pale blue dinner jackets she was unable to recognize any of the guests she had met earlier. The faces above the jackets, well beyond the circle of light, were like globs of bluish dough.

A man coughed again and Maria could hear him spit into a handkerchief above the noise of the drums. There was a rattling sound as a hand shook ice in an empty glass. The tempo of the drums increased slowly but again Maria's heart raced far ahead of the quickened beat. The blue spot changed to glaring white, forcing Maria to lower her eyes. She could not see beyond the glaring circle of light on the fleecy rug. She felt the heat of the spot on her hair.

A rude hand touched her shoulder.

She squealed with startled surprise and turned quickly around.

A tight black mask covering his eyes, a naked man stood less than two feet away. There was a reptilian smile on his lipless face.

His muscular body, shiny with olive oil, glistened saffron under the light. He reached out with his right hand, caught the neck of the flimsy net dress and, with one motion, ripped it to Maria's waist.

"Oh, no, Mr. McKay!" Maria screamed with terror above the drums. "Not him! Not him! Not him!"

She began to sob uncontrollably. As Tarzan ripped away the thin black silk covering her quivering breasts, she panicked and tried to escape. She took only two blind steps and then Tarzan imprisoned both of her thin wrists in his strong left hand. Methodically, he tore away the remaining shreds of her dress and the wide black sash beneath it. Maria squeezed her white thighs tightly together, screaming hysterically. Tarzan laughed humorlessly and with a deft sidewise kick of his bare foot knocked both of Maria's feet from under her, falling with her to the rug. He purposely released her wrists as they fell; Maria immediately raked his face and neck with her nails. She tried to bite but her teeth were unable to grip the well-greased skin of his shoulder.

"She's trying to fight him, by God," a deep male voice exclaimed proudly.

"Sure she is," another voice hoarsely replied. "That makes it all the better!"

And Maria fought, at first hysterically, and then with angry, rasping sobs; trying to bite, to kick, and to tear with her nails, as the drums pounded louder and faster. Tarzan, one hundred pounds heavier than the girl, his powerful body slippery with olive oil, easily blocked every desperate movement she made. Exhausted at last, breath whistling in her heaving lungs as she desperately gulped air through her open mouth, Maria surrendered the unequal struggle. She relaxed her body, threw her wearied arms out limply, spread her trembling legs. Her flat, chalky stomach rippled convulsively; her steaming body was drenched with perspiration. Her cinnamon-brown eyes were dark with humid hatred as she glared into Tarzan's impassive face.

Tarzan leaped lightly to his feet, lifted his jutting chin with an impatient jerk, and called: "Sanchez! Gimme a glass of water."

Sanchez entered the circle of light bearing an enamel tray holding a glass of water. Tarzan drank it thirstily, dribbling a portion over his chest, and put the glass back on the tray. Sanchez retreated unobtrusively as Tarzan wiped his damp mouth with the back of a greasy hand. As he dropped catlike to the floor again to the prostrate, sobbing girl, there exploded out of the darkness a snort of laughter.

"*Gimme a glass of water!*" the voice mimicked Tarzan's. "By God, that's rich! Really rich!"

For the next fifteen minutes, the versatile houseboy, a camera clutched in his hands, made a dozen rounds of the animated couple. When obliged to block the view of one of the pop-eyed guests, Sanchez would apologize profusely.

TWELVE

FOR Ralph, his feet tied together with a stout clothes line, wrists handcuffed behind his back, and a wide strip of adhesive tape plastered across his mouth, the night had been a long one. The concrete floor of the carport was hard. The loose ends of the clothes line had been brought up behind his back, looped and knotted to the chain between the handcuffs. He had found it impossible to rest comfortably or fall asleep.

Ralph had regained consciousness in his trussed state with a searing headache at the base of his skull. After struggling fruitlessly against his bonds for only five impatient minutes he had given up in disgust. Mosquitoes soon discovered him and covered his exposed face and neck with red burning bites. All he could do was curse to himself and shake his head to dislodge the more timid of the buzzing insects. The moonlight revealed the unmistakable silhouette of his Ford convertible, so he knew he was in the carport of the vacant house next to McKay's. The night had been humidly hot, and Ralph didn't suffer from cold, but he welcomed the first bright rays of the sun when they flooded into the wide entry ray. The well-fed mosquitoes departed with the appearance of the sun for dank breeding waters in swamps and roadside ditches.

As the sun climbed Ralph had no conception of the time. Although he tried several maneuvers with his body, he was unable to see his wristwatch. He was hungry, thirsty; his mouth was dry, and his feet were benumbed by the slow circulation of blood, caused by the tight bindings around his ankles and calves. The sharp pain in his head gradually disappeared and was replaced by a dull throbbing ache. What hurt him most, much more than mere physical discomfort, was his injured pride, and the knowledge that he had botched the "rescue" of Maria. And when they finally do get around to releasing me, if ever, he reflected hopelessly, McKay will probably have me thrown into jail for attempted housebreaking.

A few minutes later, Tarzan appeared in the doorway. Ralph had heard the grinding of gravel under the approaching footsteps, and had twisted his body around to see who was coming before the bodyguard came into view. Tarzan wore three band-aids, two on his sallow face and one on his neck. The band-aids were all in shiny blue and dotted with white stars. He wore a clean pair of cuffless khaki trousers and a blue work shirt with the sleeves cut off raggedly at the shoulders. He unhurriedly extracted a cigarette from his shirt pocket without removing the package, and scratched a kitchen match on the stucco wall. He looked down at Ralph with indifferent eyes and smoked idly for a few minutes before untying Ralph's legs. After jerking Ralph erect Tarzan had to support him until Ralph could stamp the numbness out of his feet. When Ralph could stand by himself, Tarzan turned away and started down the driveway toward the gravel road. Still handcuffed, the tape binding his mouth, Ralph stumbled along behind him. By the time they reached the front door of McKay's house, the circulation in Ralph's legs was fully restored, and he could have made a run for it, but the handcuffs behind his back discouraged him.

Sanchez opened the door for them and again Ralph followed Tarzan, who led the way across the mammoth-sized living room, through a glistening kitchen, and out the back door to the patio. McKay was seated at a wrought iron and glass table eating breakfast. He looked sorrowfully at Ralph, shook his head, and finished his glass of orange juice.

"I'm very disappointed in you, Ralph," he said disapprovingly. McKay gestured and Tarzan ripped off the adhesive tape covering Ralph's mouth with a single jerk.

"Ow!" Ralph exclaimed, hating himself for making the sharp outcry. The bodyguard tossed the piece of tape into the empty swimming pool, and sat down at the table across from his employer.

"Of course," McKay said, digging a spoon into a meaty cantaloupe, "I'm sorry this happened to you, but we thought it was a prowler. I don't believe he would have hit you with the sap if he had recognized you. Would you Tarzan?"

Tarzan grunted unintelligibly, and smeared a lavish supply of orange marmalade on a piece of toast.

"To be frank with you, Ralph," McKay continued, "your actions last night have me baffled. You sneak through the back woods there, frighten my houseboy, and then you try to batter down my front door. What did you mean by your offer to my houseboy of 'a quick twenty dollars'?"

Ralph was humiliated and ashamed and looked down at the pavement. In the bright light of early morning, his actions of the night before appeared to be infantile as well as foolish.

"I was trying to find out if Maria was out here or not," he stammered.

"I see. And you thought that if you gave my houseboy twenty dollars, he would give you this information." McKay nodded understandingly.

"Yes, sir. That's all I wanted to know."

"Tell me this then, Ralph. I think I've been fairly friendly with you in the past. Don't you think you could have obtained this information by calling me on the telephone from Miami? Or did you think I would lie to you?"

"No, sir." Ralph colored. "That isn't it at all, Mr. McKay."

"What is it then?" McKay smiled reasonably. "Are you jealous of me, a man old enough to be your father? Or are you jealous of my companion, Tarzan?"

"Haw!" Tarzan laughed.

"Was Maria out here last night?" Ralph asked.

"She was indeed," McKay said. "I had a little party and invited her to come out. There were several distinguished guests, and when she told me over the phone that she intended to stay in Miami Beach, I thought I could introduce her to some influential people as a favor. And of course, a pretty girl is always welcome at a party."

"What kind of a party was it?" Ralph blurted. "That's what I wanted to find out!"

"A party you were not invited to!" McKay snapped. He pushed his half-eaten cantaloupe to one side and called: "Sanchez! I'm ready for my eggs!"

"Me too!" Tarzan shouted.

"I believe I'm beginning to see the pattern, Ralph." McKay turned in his chair and studied Ralph's face blandly. "You knew very well Maria was here, and you intended to bribe my houseboy to take a message to her to come outside. You were jealous; resentful that she was invited and you were not. All of this stems from your failure to ride along when we took the *Sea Witch* to

Lauderdale. Come clean now, boy. Isn't that it?"

"No, sir. That isn't it."

"I am quite perturbed by your action, Ralph. If Sanchez hadn't alerted me, and if Tarzan hadn't intercepted you at the front door, I believe you would have burst into my house uninvited and created a scene. That's what I think. Perhaps you didn't notice it, but there is a sign at the entrance to the Everglades Estates stating that this area is posted. Do you know what that means?"

"Yes, sir. It means no trespassing."

"I can't decide whether to have you taken into custody or not. You can be prosecuted, fined, and spend thirty days in jail for trespassing, or did you know that?"

"Yes, sir."

"Do you want to go to jail?"

"No, sir."

"Then explain to me, in your own words, exactly what you intended to do if you had gained entrance to my home last night?"

"Nothing." Ralph colored and turned his head away.

McKay nodded to his bodyguard. Tarzan got up leisurely from the table, crossed to Ralph, and slapped him across the face with an open palm. Ralph staggered, and because he couldn't balance himself with his wrists handcuffed behind him, fell to the pavement. Tarzan returned to his seat, and Ralph scrambled clumsily to his feet again. His face smarted painfully and he could feel his cheek swelling.

"You didn't have to do that," Ralph said sullenly.

Sanchez brought a white enameled tray to the patio, and served McKay and Tarzan with a steaming plate apiece containing fried eggs, Canadian bacon, and hominy grits soaked with red-eye gravy. For the next ten minutes, McKay and his bodyguard silently ate their breakfast. Ralph looked on, shifting impatiently from one foot to the other. When he had finished eating, McKay poured a cup of coffee, added cream and sugar, and as he stirred the liquid he turned his attention to Ralph.

"I'm still waiting, Ralph."

"I wanted to talk to you personally, Mr. McKay," Ralph lied. "A fellow who used to work at the hotel came by yesterday and told me that Maria was a call girl. I was going to warn you about her."

"Maria Dugan?"

"Yes, sir. This guy also told me you were having a party, and I thought you would like to have this information. She had me completely fooled, and I didn't want you to be taken in by her. That's the reason I came out, Mr. McKay."

"Why, this is amazing, Ralph," McKay said, wrinkling his forehead. "What was the man's name who told you this?"

"I don't know his name; that is, I don't remember. It was a common name. Smith or Jones, something like that."

"This is truly amazing, Ralph," McKay said again. "It just shows that you can't judge a book by its cover. I am touched that you wanted to warn me, Ralph." He turned to the bodyguard who was looking impassively at Ralph. "Unlock his handcuffs."

Tarzan unlocked the cuffs and stuffed them into his trousers pocket. Ralph massaged his wrists, wondering what to say next. McKay pointed to the vacant chair beside him. "Sit down, Ralph, and have a cup of coffee. Get another cup for our guest," he told Tarzan.

"I don't know if it's true or not," Ralph said, sitting down gratefully. "I only heard it, you know. But I did think you ought to know about it, sir."

"She certainly fooled me, Ralph. Maria acted like a perfect lady last night. In fact, she impressed me with her manners. Most New York girls I've met down here have been poorly trained in the social graces."

Tarzan put a cup and saucer in front of Ralph, and McKay quickly filled it for him from the glass pot of coffee resting on the warmer by his elbow. Ralph helped himself to cream and sugar, and spilled two shaking spoonfuls of sugar on the glass table top before he could get a full spoonful into his cup.

"Now, I *am* sorry about what happened to you, Ralph," McKay said. "But you must admit that a telephone call would have sufficed."

"I just didn't think, sir."

"We all make mistakes and there was no real harm done. And you may be mistaken about Maria, too. I surely hope you are."

"I wouldn't accuse her unjustly, Mr. McKay," Ralph said hastily. "I only just heard it, but I thought you should know that much. In a way I felt responsible because it was me who introduced you to the girl. And I hope this guy was wrong, because I like Maria myself. I'm not in love with her, but I was sort of friendly with her. However, she did move into an apartment on the ninth floor at the Rotunda, which is suspicious."

"It certainly is, Ralph. Pretty expensive quarters for a girl who told me she wanted a typist's job."

"That's what I mean," Ralph said eagerly. "There are already a couple of hookers on Nine that I know of. That Mrs. Green and Mrs. Mattox are both—"

"Hold on, Ralph." McKay held up a hand warningly. "You're beginning to make all kinds of accusations this morning. First Maria, and now two of our permanent residents. If what you say is true, I don't know what's going on in my own hotel. Now I've met both of these ladies personally, and I've found them above reproach. Why do you accuse Mrs. Green and Mrs. Mattox of such things?"

Ralph blushed furiously. "It's common knowledge around the hotel, Mr. McKay! I thought you knew about them."

"Do you honestly believe I'd allow anything like that in my hotel, Ralph, if I knew about it?" McKay said sternly. "Why, my suite is only one floor above these ladies. How do you know that these ladies are hookers, as you so bluntly call them?"

"Well, I run the elevator at night and take men up there quite a bit. Some of them stay all night. That's a pretty good indication, isn't it?"

"Not at all, Ralph. In a room, perhaps, but an apartment is much different. Our guests are entitled to have friends in when they rent apartments, and a casual love affair with a gentleman by a permanent resident doesn't make her a common prostitute. As a college boy I thought you would be more broad-minded about such things. Haven't you ever slept with a girl you were not in love with, Ralph?"

"Yes, sir," Ralph admitted. "Maybe I've been listening to gossip that was without any true basis."

"Maybe you have at that. Listen, Ralph, you aren't one of these bitter types who hate the rich and enjoys making up malicious lies about them. You're a college boy with a summer job. But there are a lot of little people who like to carry lies about their betters. I consider you my equal, and I think I've treated you like one.

However, I'll investigate these things you've told me, and if they are true, rest assured that I'll take care of them personally. Because I have money, and you may not believe this, Ralph, I have often been the target of malicious gossip myself."

McKay stood up, stretched luxuriously, and took a wallet out of his hip pocket. He extracted a twenty-dollar bill, folded it, and handed it to Ralph.

"Take this, Ralph. In appreciation for looking after my interests."

"I don't want any money, Mr. McKay," Ralph said sincerely.

"That's why I'm giving it to you. Even though you are wrong, your heart is in the right place. But from now on, if I were you, I'd keep to myself, leave gossip to the others. You should be above such things, boy."

"I really don't deserve this money. I feel bad about taking it."

"Nonsense." McKay put a friendly arm about Ralph's shoulder. "You just keep our little conversation to yourself and I'll do some discreet investigating on my own. You keep out of hotel affairs and run your elevator. Is that sensible or not?"

"Yes, sir. It kind of looks like I made a damned fool of myself all the way around," Ralph said contritely.

"You're young, that's all. Can you drive back to town all right, or would you like Tarzan to take you in?"

"I can drive all right, sir."

"Good."

As Ralph bumped over the muddy road toward the highway he reviewed his bumbling accomplishments in his mind.

He had been a bearer of false gossip, slandering two respectable guests of the hotel. He had lied and accused Maria, a girl he was supposed to be madly in love with, of being a prostitute without any facts to back his accusations. He had believed malicious rumors about Mr. McKay, as told by a rotten male prostitute. He had almost disrupted a party of Mr. McKay's and disturbed a group of distinguished guests. And instead of firing him, putting him in jail where he rightfully belonged, Mr. McKay had tipped him twenty dollars!

How could he ever look Maria in the face after saying such things about her? How dumb could a guy get? He had readily believed every rotten thing Tommy had passed on second hand about Mr. McKay, wanted to believe it! Well, he had been slapped pretty hard across the face. That helped some. But he would have forgiven a gentleman like Mr. McKay even if Tarzan had beaten the hell out of him.

He certainly needed somebody to knock a little sense into his head!

THIRTEEN

MARIA, privately in the bathroom of her new apartment, examined her nude body with minute attention. Inside her right thigh there was a bruise the size of a saucer, with the mottled coloring of an overripe avocado. Two smaller bruises, each irregular in shape, but as big around as walnuts, were on her upper right arm. She pressed the tender bruises gingerly, but there was little pain.

I was a fool to fight him in the first place, she thought angrily. They only thought it was funny, and I added spice to their entertainment! Actually, had he wanted to, Tarzan could have really hurt her, hit her in the face with his fist, and then she would really have something to cry about this morning. A missing front tooth, for instance. Maria shuddered at the thought, slipped into her robe, and left the bathroom.

Maria counted the traveller's checks and her remaining cash. She spread the checks out in a decorative fan on the coffee table and smiled. I may bruise easy, she thought, recalling the old saying, but I heal quick!

She spread back the covers on the convertible bed-divan, pushed the button for the bed to disappear, lifted the telephone and asked for room service.

"This is Miss Dugan in 901. I want breakfast, and I'm awfully hungry. What have you got that's really good?"

"Have you tried our chef's Eggs Delmonico?" the polite voice suggested.

"What are they?"

"Very tasty, Miss Dugan. Similar to creamed eggs, but with a wonderful mushroom sauce, cheese and tiny flecks of pimento."

"All right," Maria agreed, "I'll try the Eggs Delmonico. And send up a great big pot of coffee, orange juice, and plenty of toast."

"It will be twenty minutes, maybe more, Miss Dugan."

"That's all right. Have the waiter bring me two or three movie magazines while he's at it, and the lightest shade of pancake make-up he can find in the drugstore."

Maria racked the receiver and, humming tunelessly, returned

to the bathroom to set her hair. This was a simple operation with her short hair, and she only used seven of her aluminum rollers. Finished, Maria slid the glass door to the loggia open and, sitting in the late morning sun, filed busily away at her nails, doing her best to keep her mind off last night's events.

Mr. McKay had directed Tarzan to drive her to the hotel, and she had entered the Cadillac unwillingly, but the bodyguard hadn't opened his mouth all the way back. She had sat as far away from him as possible, and when Tarzan stopped before the entrance to the Rotunda she had left the car without even saying good night. Maybe she should have been a little more friendly with him; he was only doing a job, and he had been impersonal enough. He had been the first, the very first, and all things considered, except for the initial sharp penetrating pain, he hadn't hurt her very much. Not a bit. The bruises were her own fault. Her white skin was so sensitive she had caused worse bruises by bumping into furniture and things. She sighed, and pushed back a cuticle with an orange stick. No matter how hard she tried to justify Tarzan's actions, she knew she would never be friendly with him. She had instinctively hated him when she first met him; she was afraid of him and she always would be. And that was that.

Maria had finished her breakfast and was drinking her third cup of coffee when a knock sounded at the door. It couldn't be the room waiter because she had told him she would push the table into the hall when she was through. Tossing the movie magazine to the floor, Maria opened the door and admitted a smiling Donald McKay into the room.

He winked at the girl, squeezed he arm fondly and, with a familiarity gained through past knowledge, entered the bathroom, opened the right door to the cupboard holding Maria's coffee service, and helped himself to a clean cup and saucer.

"Some people have it pretty good," McKay said teasingly as he pulled up a chair to the wheeled table and poured a cup of coffee. "Eggs Benedict for breakfast at twelve noon."

"Eggs Delmonico," Maria amended. "I never tried them before. Good, but pretty rich, I thought." She sat down at her place and lit a cigarette.

"How well do you know this fellow, Ralph Tone?" McKay frowned as he mixed cream and sugar with his coffee.

"Hardly any, Mr. McKay. Just that date on your boat is all. I've said hello to him when I rode the elevator."

"Since the date, I mean. Have you talked to him since?"

"For a few minutes. On the beach. Maybe five minutes altogether."

"Did you say anything about me?"

"I said I was staying on instead of returning to New York, and that I planned to look for a job."

"Nothing else?"

"No, sir."

"Well, I believe your friend has been smitten by your charms. He has caused me a little trouble, and I haven't quite made up my mind what to do about him. Right now, he is quite confused. I suppose at one time I was as young as he is—never *quite* as young—but young anyway. How old do you suppose Ralph is, Maria?"

"He told me he was twenty-five."

"That much? Well, now, that's interesting. Lately all young men from eighteen to twenty-seven or so look about the same to me."

"Not to me, Mr. McKay," Maria laughed, and blushed prettily.

"No, I guess not. You kind of like Ralph yourself, don't you?"

"He's very nice, I thought. He's going to college, and he has a marvelous personality."

"You wouldn't mind having him make love to you then?"

"I didn't say that!" Maria blushed again and looked away.

"I know. *I* said it. One of the gentlemen last night took a fancy to you, Maria, and tonight I'm going to pair you off with him—"

"So soon? I thought..." Maria's voice trailed off with embarrassment.

"What did you think?" McKay said sharply.

"I really don't know what I thought," she said honestly.

"That's better. I'll do all of the thinking. And I think that I'm going to try a little experiment with Ralph. Before tonight, let's see if we can sandwich Ralph in, too. Give you a little practice, and maybe teach Ralph a lesson in the facts of life."

"You mean...let Ralph make love to me?" Maria faltered.

"Not exactly let him." McKay smiled picaresquely. "We'll let him pay! From now on, Maria, everybody pays."

"I couldn't do that, Mr. McKay!" Maria exclaimed. "Ralph is more like a friend, and it would be too personal. I don't want him to know about me, about what I'm doing. With a stranger it's different. I mean—"

"I know what you mean. I also know we can take Ralph for about three hundred dollars. One-fifty to be yours, of course. We aren't dealing in scruples, Maria. We work on a cash basis. And as I said, I want to experiment with this high-minded youth. He caused me a bad moment of anxiety, and my rather warped set of principles is involved."

"If it's all the same to you, Mr. McKay, I'd rather not," Maria said flatly.

"Do you think it's wise to disagree with me, my dear?" McKay looked calmly at Maria, studying her face curiously. Maria lifted her chin defiantly, stared back for a moment, and then dropped her eyes to the plate in front of her. She snuffed out her cigarette in the gooey remains of her breakfast.

"No, sir," she replied in a small voice.

"All right." McKay took a slip of paper out of his wallet and handed it to Maria. "This is Ralph's telephone number. Call him and have him meet you here this afternoon. Three o'clock should be a good time. It'll be much easier than you think. He already suspects that you're in the call girl business, whatever that is."

"But how—" Maria said quickly, "I mean, who could have told him?"

"In a hotel, Maria, the employees know everything that goes on." McKay finished the last of his coffee and stood up. "Well, this has been very pleasant, but I have to go. I'll have Tarzan pick you up downstairs at eight tonight. What are you going to wear?"

"I have a white silk cocktail gown. Is that all right?"

"It'll do for tonight. Better buy some evening dresses in the next few days. Charge them if you like; you'll be able to pay for them. Business is excellent for offseason, but this winter it will be much better." McKay crossed to the door, turned with his hand on the knob. "Don't just sit there, Maria! I said to telephone Ralph!"

"Yes, sir," Maria said guiltily, getting quickly to her feet. The door slammed, and Maria sat down again, looking wistfully at the crumpled slip of paper in her hand.

As three o'clock approached, Maria grew increasingly apprehensive concerning Ralph's impending visit. She had covered the large bruise on her thigh and the smaller bruises on her arm with make-up, but they were still pink blotches against her white skin. She wore a long-sleeved blue frock, and wore it over her naked body, without the restraint of brassiere, panties or slip. A wide red belt around her waist matched her lipstick, and she wore her white, high-heeled pumps without stockings. After Maria had taken the curlers out of her hair, she had rehearsed in her mind a dozen methods of propositioning Ralph, and had discarded every one of them as either too crude or too coarse. Ralph's landlady had reluctantly called Ralph to the telephone, but he had accepted eagerly when she invited him to come to her apartment for a drink at three. But now that three was close at hand, what would she do when he arrived?

The apartment looked wonderful; the maid had done a quick but efficient job of cleaning, and there was a fresh bowl of red roses on the cocktail table in front of the divan. Maria had filled an aluminum bucket with ice cubes, and had closed the glass door to the loggia to allow the air-conditioning to cool the room. Wishing that she had one of those yellow capsules to take that Helen had given her, Maria fixed a stiff drink of scotch with very little soda instead, and downed it hurriedly. Setting down the empty glass, Maria lifted the telephone for the third time in a half-hour and asked the operator for the time.

"Two forty-five," the operator said patiently.

"Thank you."

As she replaced the receiver, Ralph knocked timidly at the door.

Maria had a definite advantage over Ralph although she was not aware of it. The advantage was that of hotel guest over hotel employee. When he had taken Maria on their date in his car, meeting her outside the hotel, he had been perfectly comfortable. But to visit Maria in a $250 a week apartment in the same hotel where he was employed as an elevator operator was something else altogether. While Maria had nervously awaited his arrival, Ralph had waited himself for more than an hour in the employee's locker room. To keep his clothes as fresh as possible he had brought his suit, shirt and tie to the hotel, taken a shower there and dressed in the basement. Too restless to wait any longer he had taken the service elevator to the ninth floor fifteen minutes ahead of time and, after lighting a cigarette, had rapped hesitantly at the door to 901.

Ralph entered shyly, pushed the door closed behind him, and smiled boyishly at Maria.

"How nice you look!" both of them said in unison. The tension in the room dissolved immediately as they both laughed. Maria turned toward the bar and said over her shoulder: "Sit down, Ralph. A scotch and soda all right?"

"Fine. Not too much soda." Ralph sat down on the first third of the divan and pulled up his trousers at the knee. His suit was of pale lightweight gray Dacron, and he wore black shoes, a black knit tie, and gray silk socks.

Maria sat down beside him, handed him a tall drink, and leaned forward to take a cigarette from the package on the coffee table. She leaned forward deliberately to expose the cleavage of her full, unhampered breasts, and Ralph was duly impressed. He took his lighter out of his coat pocket and, as he raised it to Maria's cigarette, she held tightly to his wrist with both hands.

"And here we are!" Maria said brightly. She drank half her highball before setting the glass down on the low table.

"Yes," Ralph agreed heartily. "That's right!"

"How do you like my apartment, Ralph?"

"Very nice." He looked around the room. "I suppose it's pleasant to sit out on the loggia in the evening?"

"Oh, yes! A marvelous view."

Ralph finished his highball in three quick swallows, rattled the ice in the empty glass. "Are you about ready for another?" Maria finished her drink quickly and nodded.

Ralph mixed two more drinks at the small bar. "This is good scotch, Maria," he remarked pleasantly.

"Is it? I don't know one brand from another. It tastes all right, though."

"Excellent scotch."

Without more small talk, they finished their fresh drinks as though they were being paid to drink and were being paid by the glass. Maria set her empty glass beside Ralph's on the table, and faced him with a serious face.

"I want to be kissed, Ralph," she stated flatly.

"Well, I guess I can do it," Ralph said smilingly. He took Maria into his arms and she pressed her breasts against him, moving her shoulders back and forth, burrowing into his chest. She opened her mouth wide, forcing her tongue between his lips, and they clung together, scarcely breathing. Almost carelessly, Maria dropped her hand into Ralph's lap, and gently began to caress his thigh.

Ralph broke away from Maria's demanding mouth, pushed her gently away, and got to his feet. His face was flushed beneath his tan, and his eyes were bright with excitement. Ralph took off his jacket, arranged it neatly over the back of a chair, and loosened his tie. He sat down again and reached for the girl, but Maria stood up. The table was then between them. She looked down at Ralph's face and pursed her lips thoughtfully.

"Do you want me, Ralph?" she asked seriously.

"What a question!" Ralph exclaimed, leaping to his feet and starting around the table.

"Sit down, Ralph!" Maria's voice was sharp, and she backed away from him.

Shrugging his shoulders, Ralph returned obediently to his seat and looked questioningly at Maria's pensive face. He was completely puzzled by the girl's sudden coldness after the abandon of her passionate kiss.

"I mean, Ralph," a tiny line formed between her arched brows, "do you really want me?"

"I love you, Maria," Ralph said simply. "I want you more than anything in the world." His voice was choked and his hands trembled. And he tightened them into fists.

Maria sat down across from Ralph and looked at him curiously. How easily she had aroused him. She sat stiffly, her tense body hard and tough as steel. She felt nothing inside except an icy cold. This was a business. I am a commodity, and they must pay. All of them, including Ralph...Mr. McKay was right.

"I'm glad to hear you say that, Ralph," Maria said bluntly. "Because I'm all yours for three hundred dollars. Cash, of course, and paid in advance."

Maria realized that her words were cruel and crudely spoken, but she was totally unprepared for Ralph's reaction to them. He didn't get angry; he didn't shout or scream at her or dash angrily for the door. He looked at her steadily, dully, and then his lips trembled, and slow tears welled out of his eyes. He didn't wipe them away. He cried soundlessly, his shoulders shaking with disillusioned grief. Maria was almost caught by Ralph's shameless distress, but hardened herself quickly. Angrily she snatched her glass from the table and mixed a drink at the bar.

"Well, what did you expect?" she said heartlessly, her rigid back to Ralph. "How do you think I pay for an apartment like this? I've worked all over," she lied. "Las Vegas, New York. What are you, anyway? Some high school letterman who thinks he can get it free because he's good-looking or something?"

A moment later, Maria heard the chain lock rattle as Ralph opened the door, but she didn't turn around. She stared blindly into her full glass, waiting for the door to slam. That was that. She could tell Mr. McKay she had tried and failed. He couldn't expect anymore from her than that...

"Maria?" Ralph said quietly.

"Yes."

"I'll be right back. Give me a half-hour to raise the money."

"All right, Ralph. I'll be waiting."

"And I'll have the money." There wasn't a trace of anger or bitterness in his soft voice.

Maria didn't touch her fresh drink. When the door clicked shut she went to the loggia, and leaned over the concrete wall, looking out to sea. She knew Ralph would be back, and then every link with respectability would be destroyed. And she knew with intense quiet pain that it didn't have to be like this. She could just as easily have made Ralph propose marriage to her. But after last night there was no turning back. Ralph had offered her his friendship on the beach, and just now he had offered his love, and she had erased both friendship and love by a brutal request for money. When Ralph came back with the money it would be money had couldn't actually afford to pay, and only half of it would belong to her.

Ralph was back within twenty-five minutes, knocking confidently at the door. There was no deference in the manner of Ralph's second entrance into Maria's apartment; he entered boldly, crossed directly to his coat which he had left behind, and took his lighter and cigarettes out of his pocket. He lit a cigarette, pulled out his wallet, and busily counted out rumpled bills on the coffee table. He even managed a bit of levity, laughing dryly and cocking his head humorlessly as he grinned sardonically at Maria.

"You broke me, kid," he said, "but you're worth a thousand dollars to me. It could have cost me my entire life. This hundred and twenty represents my bank account. This twenty is a little tip from our mutual friend, Mr. Donald McKay. Forty more is my terminal pay, but I've wanted to quit my lousy job anyway. Ten I had, and the rest was garnered from the savings of my esteemed fraternity brother. Count it, Maria, every dirty dollar! Three hundred even."

Maria picked up the loose bills. "All right, Ralph, I'll—"

"Don't call me Ralph. I am *Mr.* Tone to you! When I pay this kind of money I belong to the 'yes, sir' and 'no, sir' class."

"As you prefer it, Mr. Tone," Maria said uneasily. She counted the money, jammed it carelessly into her purse, and moved the coffee table away from the divan. Ralph mixed another drink and sat down in an armchair against the wall as Maria pushed the button to bring the double bed out of the divan. She turned back the covers, and smoothed the sheet with fluttering fingers.

"Well..." Maria cleared her throat.

"Everything ready?" Ralph said with an amused smile.

"Any time you are."

"I'm not in any big hurry, Maria. Let me see what I've bought. Go ahead. Show me," he ordered sternly as she stood hesitantly before him.

Maria forced herself to strut about the room, tried to behave provocatively, to display herself. Her face was flushed in both girlish modesty and sullen anger. Ralph twisted in his chair and, still seated, unscrewed the lamp shade from the table lamp on the end table. He switched on the bright glove, and crooked his forefinger at Maria.

"A little closer, sweetheart," he said. "I want to take a good look."

Maria advanced to within two feet of Ralph's chair and stopped. He raised her dress, looked closely at her quivering thighs and discovered the large bruise beneath the pink make-up.

"What's this?" Ralph asked, kneading her thigh gently with thumb and fingers.

"It's a bruise," Maria replied angrily, stepping back a pace. "I bumped into a table!"

"Turn around."

Completely humiliated, Maria whirled about and stood as before, with her heels tight together. Ralph prodded her tense buttocks with rude, stiff fingers. "Front again," he ordered.

Ralph got to his feet, put the unfinished drink on the end table, and snuffed out his cigarette in the ashtray. He cupped and lifted Maria's right breast, and then the left, nodding thoughtfully.

"You don't have any disease, do you?" he asked politely.

"No!" Maria shouted, her eyes glowing with fierce resentment.

"No, *sir*, Maria," Ralph reminded her chidingly. "I'm a very good customer, you know."

"No, sir." Maria swallowed, turned her flaming face away from Ralph's businesslike examination of her body.

"That's better. A young man can't be too careful, you know. Lot of things going around Florida these days. Asian Flu, sputniks, wheels, nuts and bolts, athlete's foot, old retired couples without driver's licenses..."

Ralph lay on the bed, putting both of the pillows comfortably beneath his head. He looked contemplatively at the ceiling, and crossed his ankles.

"Okay, Maria," he said after a long moment. "Go ahead, make love to me. I'm paying for it, not you."

"What do you want me to do?"

"Sir!"

"Sir."

"Don't you know?"

"It's up to you...sir."

"Not for three hundred dollars. It's up to you!"

Timidly, fearfully, Maria got on her hands and knees and kissed Ralph's hard, tight mouth, his neck, his cheeks, and lightly ran her fingers over his chest. Ralph continued to gaze at the ceiling, his brown eyes as hard as volcanic glass.

And then a hard, dry sob issued from Maria's parched throat. She turned away from Ralph, and dropped flat on the bed. She buried her face in the sheet, sobbing hopelessly, uncontrollably. She felt the springs rise as Ralph got up, but she kept her face hidden, unable to stop crying.

Ralph finally patted her on the shoulder. "Here," he said kindly, "drink this."

Maria sat up on the edge of the bed, rubbing her wet face with her fingers, and accepted the double shot of scotch Ralph gave her. Ralph mopped her face with the end of a damp face towel. Maria gulped down the raw whiskey and coughed. She blinked at the floor, too ashamed to raise her eyes.

"You're a phoney, Maria," Ralph said calmly. "I wasn't sure, but I had to find out. You don't know a damned thing. Nothing. No, I'm not a young high school boy who expects to get it free. I've been around and I've had to pay for it, and they aren't like you, Maria. You thought I was rough on you, but I wasn't rough at all. That wasn't even the standard treatment that most prostitutes get." Ralph took Maria's empty glass, got her robe from the closet, and tossed it on the foot of the bed.

"Here, put this on and cover yourself," he said gruffly.

"I'm sorry, Ralph," Maria said, putting on her robe and typing the belt. She still kept her eyes from Ralph's face.

"You're mixed up with McKay, aren't you?"

Maria nodded in reply.

"Come on," Ralph ordered. "Get dressed, throw your clothes in a bag, and let's get out of here. My car's downstairs. By tomorrow morning we'll be in South Carolina, halfway to New York."

"No," Maria shook her head. "I can't."

"Why can't you?"

"I can't!"

"You mean you won't."

"I can't. It's too late," she said hopelessly.

"It's never too late."

"I won't go, that's all. Goodbye, Ralph," Maria said woodenly.

"Do you have any idea what it's like? Don't you realize what you're getting into?"

"Yes, I do know. And I don't care."

"Nothing I can say or do will change your mind?"

"No. Just go away and leave me alone."

"All right, Maria." Ralph took his three hundred dollars out of Maria's purse, counted it, and put the money into his wallet. He wadded his knit tie, stuffed it into his coat pocket, and draped his light jacket over his right shoulder, hooking his thumb in the neckband.

"You're lost, Maria," he said. "Lost forever."

"I know it, and I don't give a damn."

"It could have been different." Ralph slammed the door behind him.

As soon as the door was closed, Maria shot the bolt, ran into the bathroom and anxiously examined her face in the mirror. Her eyelids were red and swollen. She soaked a clean washrag in water as hot as she could stand it and feverishly bathed her swollen face. She wanted to look her very best for the party, and she only had until eight o'clock to get ready.

How mean Ralph was to take his money back! What could she possibly tell Mr. McKay?

FOURTEEN

RALPH rode the service elevator down to the basement, clanged the door shut, and walked down the concrete corridor toward the employee's locker room, his slow footsteps echoing hollowly in the passageway. Johnny Townsend, who had finished his tour of elevator duty, was sitting on the bench in front of the row of lockers, lacing a pair of brown and white oxfords. When Johnny saw Ralph, he smiled with pleased surprise.

"What are you doing down here, Ralph? I thought you were sunburned so bad you couldn't work!" He laughed.

"I came down to quit," Ralph replied, working the combination of his locker.

"No kidding?"

"That's right, Johnny." Ralph spread a dirty white shirt on the floor and dumped items from his locker onto the shirt. He handed six paperbacked, twenty-five cent novels to Johnny. "Something to read in the elevator, kid."

"What're you going to do now, Ralphie?"

"I don't know," Ralph replied truthfully. "I haven't looked that far ahead."

"If you get a daytime job, Ralphie, call me. We can go out together some night. I've never seen so much loose stuff running around in my whole life! And all these girls have money to spend on handsome young fellows like me and you. Miami Beach sure ain't like Michigan, boy!" Townsend was dressed in a skin-tight pair of blue jeans, and a screaming red short-sleeved sport shirt. His light hair, still wet from the shower, tumbled over his forehead.

"I'll keep in touch, John. That is, if I stay in Miami. Will you do me a favor before you go?"

"Sure, Ralph. Unless you need dough. I don't have any," Johnny said cheerfully, turning his empty pockets inside out to prove it.

"Go up to the dining room for me and ask Tom Grant to come down a minute. I'd go myself, but Old Sourball is still pretty sore at me."

"All right, I'll tell Tommy to come down. You don't suppose Old Sourball will grab me off as your replacement, do you?"

Townsend asked anxiously.

"No, I doubt it. And if he does you don't have to work a double shift. You just got off, so in effect you'd be working three shifts in a row. So he can't make you take my place."

"If I see him I'll dodge anyway." Johnny pushed open the door, and Ralph heard his running feet in the corridor.

Most of the accumulation in Ralph's locker was trash, and he dumped what he didn't want into the empty metal barrel by the outside door. His swimming trunks, three pairs of stiff, dirty socks, a mildewed canvas shaving kit, four dirty T-shirts, and a large white bath towel, plainly marked ROTUNDA HOTEL in red block letters, were all he kept. He tied the small bundle together with the shirt-sleeves of the dirty white shirt.

Ralph sat down on the bench to smoke while he waited for Tommy. Two bald middle-aged bartenders entered the locker room from the back and began to change their clothes. Ralph examined their dour faces with the dawning realization that all of the bartenders he had ever known looked exactly like these two. Not that they were all bad, although most of them were, at that, but their expressions were all alike. All face, like character actors in the movies; expressive eyebrows, small chins, and large liquid eyes. Ralph pictured these two men later working behind the bar, changing their expression to match the mood of each customer at the busy half-price cocktail hour in the Rotunda Lounge. But right now, in repose, their characterless expressions oddly reminded Ralph of ex-Presidents born in Ohio.

"I took Mr. Reese for three-fifty last night," the first bartender remarked tonelessly.

"Yeah. On change for a twenty or a fifty you can take Mr. Reese every time." His companion pouted thoughtfully. "That's what he deserves for drinking stingers."

The two bartenders, in white stiffly-starched jackets, red bowties, and faded maroon trousers, pushed through the swinging doors and marched quietly into the corridor on rubber-soled feet. If I stayed in hotel work for twenty years, Ralph reflected, I'd look exactly like them some day. Bartenders on the five P.M. to three A.M. shift had the best-paying jobs in the hotel. Any hotel...

Deep in thought, Ralph didn't hear his roommate enter the room. "How'd you make out, Ralph?" Tommy said, clapping

Ralph on the shoulder.

Ralph picked up his bundle, looked soberly at his friend. "Let's go out to my car where we can talk, Tom."

"Okay, but not too long. I've got to get back to work."

As soon as they were seated in the car, Ralph took out his billfold and counted $110.00 into Tommy's hand. Tommy folded the money and put it into his trousers pocket, twisting sideways in the seat.

"Maria was a phoney, Tom. An amateur." Ralph explained. "If she got into the racket she must have only started last night at McKay's party. They probably got her drunk or something like that. I don't know. And I don't know why she picked on me, either. Practice, maybe. A bright idea that she could pick up a fast three hundred bucks without McKay finding out about it. Hell, I don't know."

"You didn't go through with it, then?" Tommy asked softly.

"I intended to, but I couldn't. Somehow, I kept seeing our old girl friend, Hazel, in that ratty shack. Maria doesn't realize yet, Tommy, just what she's letting herself in for. I tried to talk to her, but I couldn't get through. She knows she's wrong, but evidently the money looks so damned big to her she can't think of anything else. I don't know what to do, but I have to do something."

"I thought I knew you pretty well, Ralph, but you're acting without thinking. You quit your job without saying anything to me. Hell, I could have cashed a check for the whole three hundred just as easy as one-ten. You know that!"

"I know." Ralph turned earnestly to his friend. "I'd have quit anyway, Tommy. Do you think I could've run that elevator every night, knowing what was going on? Every time I took a man to the ninth floor I'd have followed him to see if he went into 901. And if he did, I'd be half-crazy until he came out again!"

"She isn't worth it, Ralph. If I were in love with a woman and she tried to nick me for three hundred bucks the way Maria did you I'd kick her teeth in! Do you honestly love her after a trick like that?"

"I don't know. I don't know how I feel about her. She's so damned dumb, Tommy! But every woman I've ever known was dumb, so I don't hold that against her. I can't analyze how I feel. I'm tired. I've been awake all night, and I've had a hell of a shock besides. When she called me at noon I had just gotten into bed.

And after she called, I felt like an iron band had been taken off my chest. Then I couldn't sleep. And now my whole body feels like a big chunk of ice buried under a ton of sawdust."

Tommy bit his upper lip worriedly. "You shouldn't be by yourself, Ralph, not in the mood you're in," he said seriously. "And if you start poking your nose into McKay's affairs, you'll wind up floating in Biscayne Bay minus your head. I mean it, Ralph!"

"I never saw a guy like McKay before." Ralph shook his head disbelievingly. "He's practiced lying so long he must believe his own lies. I believed him. He worked my brain up and down like a yoyo, and I accepted everything he said at face value."

Tommy punched Ralph affectionately on the arm. "Okay, then, buddy. Keep out of McKay's way. Go on home and stay there. When I come in tonight, we'll go out and have a few beers and talk things out. You can get another job or we can go up to Orlando and make concrete bricks for your old man. If that doesn't suit you, we can go to my place in Valdosta and play golf every day at the country club. We've got the rest of the summer, Ralph, and by the time school starts you'll forget you ever met Maria."

"You're a damned good friend, Tommy," Ralph said sincerely. "Go on back to work. And on your way, stop at the desk and look up Peggy Vittorni's forwarding address for me. Call me at home. I'll be waiting by the phone."

"Now what are you going to do?" Tommy said without hiding his exasperation.

"I'm going to call New York. Miss Vittorni. Tell her what Maria's getting into, and tell her to contact Maria's family."

"What good will that do? Maria's a grown woman, Ralph—"

"If you don't want to get me the address I'll get it myself. How I feel about Maria isn't the important thing anymore. I was the one who introduced her to McKay. If it wasn't for me, she'd be home right now, and as you said, by the end of summer I'd have forgotten I ever met her."

Tommy opened the door and got out, slammed it shut, and nodded. "Go ahead, Ralph. I'll get the address and call within a half hour. But promise me you'll stay in the room until I get in tonight."

"Sure." Ralph switched on the ignition, punched the starter, and the engine roared into life. As the door to the locker room closed behind Tommy Grant, the *maitre d' hotel* rushed out of the kitchen exit, looked up and down the alley searching anxiously for his Head Busboy. By the time the *maitre d'* returned to the dining room, Tommy would be busily slicing butter as though he had been there all the time.

Ralph shot out of the parking lot and turned into the swiftly-moving traffic stream of the highway.

To allow Peggy Vittorni plenty of time to get home from work, Ralph didn't call New York until seven-thirty. He called from a pay booth, inside a neighborhood drugstore, three blocks away from his rooming house. The call went through immediately, and Ralph dropped the required change into the slot. To prepare for overtime, he had lined up five dollars in quarters, stacking them in sets of four on the narrow metal shelf.

"Is that you, Maria?" A high feminine voice crackled in his ear.

"No. This is Ralph Tone."

"Who?"

"Ralph Tone. You might remember me. Night elevator man at the Rotunda Hotel."

"Oh, yes. Let me speak to Maria, please."

"Maria isn't here. This is Peggy Vittorni, isn't it?"

"Who else would it be? Where is Maria? Has anything happened to her?" the voice asked anxiously.

"No," Ralph said. "She's fine. I only called to tell you that Maria's mixed up in some trouble down here—"

"Trouble? What's that again, please?"

"What I mean is..." Ralph took time out to wipe his perspiring face with his handkerchief. "Miss Vittorni?"

"Yes, I can hear you."

"Maria's gotten into some bad company, and I thought you ought to know about it. Gangsters."

The voice snorted angrily, painfully, into Ralph's ear. "What is this, Ralph? Some kind of gag?"

"No. I'm serious about this," Ralph faltered. "She's in serious trouble, and she's getting in over her head. I thought that—"

"All right. You've had your fun, Ralph. Put Maria on the phone now," the voice said icily.

"I'm very serious about this!" Ralph said loudly. "Just listen a minute. Maria is mixed up with a very bad element in Miami, and I called you because you're supposed to be her friend. If you are Maria's friend, contact her folks and have them persuade her to come home."

"Is that all? Can't you give me any details?"

"I can, yes. But not over the telephone. I only want to impress on you that I'm serious and mean what I say."

"I can tell you're serious all right."

"Will you contact her folks then?"

"Right away. Now put Maria on, please."

"She isn't here. I'm calling from a drugstore. Can't you get it through your thick skull that—" There was a click followed by a steady humming tone, and Ralph didn't complete his sentence. He punched open the folding door, scraped the five piles of quarters into his hand, and wiped his face again with his damp handkerchief. The drugstore was air-conditioned, and to cool off more he sat down at the fountain and ordered a large soda.

What an idiot Peggy is, he though disgustedly. By the time he finished his soft drink he was in a more reasonable frame of mind. Suppose the conditions had been reversed? Suppose Peggy Vittorni had called him from New York and informed him that his buddy, Tommy Grant, was mixed up with gangsters? Would he have taken the call seriously? Maybe. Maybe not. But then, he knew that Tommy wasn't the type to get mixed up with gangsters.

Ralph laughed suddenly.

Miss Vittorni "knew" that Maria wasn't the type to get mixed up with gangsters, either. If he had told Miss Vittorni in the beginning that Maria was a practicing prostitute, the call wouldn't have lasted as long as it had.

He ordered another soda.

If Maria was to be saved from herself, he would have to do it. How, he didn't know, but somehow. Seven or eight years ago, Hazel had probably started out like Maria was doing now, and he couldn't let that happen. The memory of Hazel's bloated face, her lumpy hips, and the light in her eyes when she had snatched the bottle of scotch from his hands, popped vividly into his mind.

Ralph dropped a quarter and a dime on the marble counter and left the drugstore.

FIFTEEN

BY seven forty-five, Maria was dressed and ready, waiting in the downstairs lobby for McKay's bodyguard to pick her up. Her pale ivory face was serene and beautiful. In her white silk gown, sitting patiently in a rose-colored chair, she had a regal bearing, the confident poise of the attractive woman who is well aware of her good looks and does not have to be reassured.

If Maria felt any inner tension she did not show it in her outward demeanor. The tear-ravaged face of the afternoon had been repaired; and the aftereffects of the scotch she had consumed during the scene with Ralph had been eliminated in a long, lingering, well-scented bath. The persistent queasiness in her stomach, caused by fear and thoughts of her own inadequacy concerning what would happen when she retired to a bedroom with an unknown "guest," had been partially allayed by eating a thick sirloin steak in her room. A young woman like Maria Dugan, with a full stomach and a purse containing several hundred dollars, could not allow herself to dwell on the unpleasant aspects of the evening ahead. Why not, Maria thought, a beatific smile lighting her features, think instead of all the wonderful things the money will buy?

"Hi, honey!" Helen said. "Ready?"

"Oh, it's you!" Maria got up immediately. Helen wore a stark, black sheath of silk, so simply designed that any determined woman shopper could buy one exactly like it for eight hundred dollars. Her fine blonde hair was piled high on her head, lacquered expertly into place, and two unevenly shaped pieces of jade dangled from her pierced ears. On the third finger, left hand, Helen wore another piece of mottled jade the size and approximate shape of a squashed ping pong ball, set into a wide band of filigreed silver. A black beaded bag looped down from the crook of her left elbow on a long silken cord.

"How beautiful you look, Helen!" Maria exclaimed.

"You look mighty sweet yourself," Helen replied warmly.

Arm in arm, the two young women swept through the lobby, out of the door, and joined Tarzan in the front seat of the yellow Cadillac convertible. Maria dropped back, allowing Helen the dubious privilege of sitting by the unshaven, seedy bodyguard. Tarzan wheeled into the traffic stream, and pointed the car for the Everglades Estates.

"It's just you and me tonight, Maria," Helen said. "Only two guests."

"I'm glad it's you that's with me," Maria whispered.

Helen patted Maria's knee in reply. There were several questions Maria would have liked to ask her companion, but Tarzan's forbidding presence in the driver's seat inhibited her. Listening to the radio, the trio rode without further conversation to McKay's home in the Everglades Estates.

As soon as they entered the living room, McKay drew Maria aside, while Tarzan and Helen accompanied Sanchez into the kitchen for coffee. Following her employer down the hallway, Maria entered a small study as McKay directed.

"Sit down, Maria," McKay said pleasantly, pulling a chair up close to his neat desk. "I had you come out early tonight because of some paperwork you must sign."

Maria sat down, looking puzzledly at McKay as he seated himself in a swivel hair behind the desk.

"Paperwork?" she asked.

"Yes, the usual administrative claptrap." McKay opened a legal-sized Manila folder, passed printed forms and a pen to Maria. "Sign on the lines I've marked with a little X. The first one is your Workman's Compensation Act form, and the small one is for withholding tax; and here is the Social Security folder. Have you got your Social Security card with you?"

"I think so," Maria replied. She opened her purse, and finally found her card in a small leather case. "Here it is." She passed the card to McKay and he copied the number into a thick, leather-covered notebook. Maria signed her name on the forms in the required spaces and returned the pen to McKay.

"I agreed to work for you," Maria said, wetting her lips, "but all these forms have me confused. I mean, what am I supposed—"

"Hostess. You're listed as hostess. Nothing else. And your salary is seventy-five dollars a week. Everything else is clear and above board, my dear. I wanted to explain a few simple procedures, as I said, but don't be alarmed. The law is the law, you know. For instance, open a bank account, but don't deposit more than seventy-five dollars a week. Rent a safe-deposit box, and hide the rest of your money in it. Looks mighty suspicious for a woman to deposit more than she earns. And spend from your bank account once in awhile. You're supposed to be living on your salary."

"In a two hundred and fifty a week apartment?" Maria raised arched eyebrows.

"Technically, I pay for your room, Maria. On the books, I provide your living quarters, but you actually pay me personally in cash from your earnings."

"I see. When can I move to a cheaper place?"

"When I say so, my dear," McKay smiled pleasantly. "In the off season it isn't easy to rent efficiencies, and I don't like to have them standing empty. The loss of revenue is very depressing. When the season starts, and if business is good, you can either move or pay the higher seasonal rates. What's the matter, Maria? Don't you like your new quarters?"

"That isn't the idea, Mr. McKay. I wasn't complaining, but the rent is so expensive, I don't see how I'm going to save anything."

"It's a little early to talk about hoarding money, isn't it? Now, how did the matinee affair go with Mr. Tone?"

"Well..." Maria blushed twisted the handbag in her lap. "Not so good, Mr. McKay!" she blurted.

"I'm surprised, really surprised. I seldom guess wrong on a client. Couldn't he raise the money?" McKay clasped his hands behind his head, looked thoughtfully at the ceiling. "Three o'clock was too late. One o'clock would have been better, I believe. Give him more time to raise the money. What do you think?"

"He had the money all right, Mr. McKay...but afterwards, he took it back...." She looked down at the white toes of her shoes. "He said I wasn't worth three hundred dollars," she whispered.

"Don't worry about it, my dear, because I know you are. If Ralph welched on the deal, it's my fault. I considered the possibility, but I misjudged him. I thought Ralph was a high-minded young man." McKay sighed, shook his head sorrowfully. "This is a lesson to us both. You can never take anybody for granted in this business. But I'll see what I can do."

"I'm sorry, Mr. McKay."

"Don't be. The collection of fees is my province, and I'll take care of it. Now let's join the others."

Under a wealth of candlelight, a small, intimate table for five had been set up in the living room. Resting on spidery tripods, two silver buckets containing shaved ice and bottles of champagne flanked both sides of the table. The table had been set for a late evening supper, and the food had been attractively arranged by the meticulous houseboy. There was a huge, steaming silver bowl containing a smooth and tasty Welsh rarebit; a large white platter of toast points with the crusts removed; a lazy susan circular tray in the middle of the table with assorted relishes, and five individual crystal bowls brimming with fresh fruit salad, topped with great globs of whipped cream.

At the head of the table, Donald McKay discoursed at length on possible Republican candidates for the presidency in the next election, while the two gentlemen guests, both of them introduced to Helen and Maria as "Mr. Smith," listened attentively. Maria and Helen sat across from each other, on the right and left of McKay respectively, and when an opportunity presented itself, Helen would wink at the younger girl and jerk her head toward McKay as if to say, "Listen to who is talking, will you?" Every time Helen made this gesture, Maria giggled helplessly, and McKay would frown before continuing.

Maria's companion, seated at her right elbow, reminded her of an oversized bull frog. He was bald, except for a thin fringe of silvery hair, and his bloated red face was criss-crossed just beneath the surface with hundreds of tiny blue lines. White shaggy eyebrows shaded his tiny eyes, which were deeply recessed in their sockets, and in the candlelight, Maria was unable to tell whether his eyes were blue, green or gray. In a black silk dinner jacket, his crisp, white shirt front and old-fashioned white piquéd vest made him appear as wide as he was tall. Why, he must be in his seventies, at least, she had thought when they had been introduced. In high heels, Maria towered more than a foot above her guest, but he made up for his shortness of stature by outweighing her more than 150 pounds.

Helen's "Mr. Smith" was of middle height, but appeared slim and tall in contrast to Maria's partner. A man in his early sixties, he still retained considerable side hair, and he had allowed these side locks to grow long, and then combed them sideways over his bare pink skull. However, he obviously wasn't well. His long wrinkled hands trembled constantly; there were nervous tics in both wrinkled cheeks, and when Sanchez had placed the silver bowl of Welsh rarebit on the table, he had accused Mr. McKay of trying to poison him. He had ungraciously refused McKay's solicitous offer of anything else and confined himself to sipping distastefully and suspiciously at his glass of champagne.

If Maria had been given her choice of the two gentlemen by McKay, which, of course, she had not been given, she wouldn't have willingly chosen either one. She had attempted to fortify herself against the forthcoming night in the bedroom by drinking champagne as rapidly as possible, but after an uncomfortably pro-longed giggle, caused by Helen's broad wink, McKay had cut her off from the supply by an unseen signal to the hovering Sanchez.

"Perhaps you gentlemen would like to see some movies," Mr. McKay suggested after Sanchez had cleared the table. "I received an excellent animated cartoon, by courier, which was made in Mexico City. I found it very amusing."

"I didn't fly fifteen hundred miles to see a movie," Maria's guest croaked, squeezing her knee surreptitiously beneath the table with soft, pudgy fingers.

"Of course not," McKay said pleasantly. "But while the girls re-tire to their rooms, we may as well enjoy a cigar and a demitasse, and examine the cartoon as well. I assure you, gentlemen, you will find it both educational and entertaining."

Helen pushed her chair back, stood up, and crooked a finger at Maria. The two young women excused themselves, and made their exit from the living room into the hallway. Helen took Maria's arm at the elbow, and whispered for her to follow into Number Four.

"How are you, Maria?" Helen asked, once they were inside the brilliantly-lighted bedroom. "Do you feel all right?"

"Nervous is all. Why wouldn't Sanchez pour me any more champagne? I asked him three times," Maria pouted.

"Mr. McKay cut you off, but it's better, believe me. It doesn't pay to get drunk on these parties. Would you like one of those yellow capsules, like I gave you last night?"

"No, I don't think so. Just tell me what I should do when I'm alone with Mr. Smith."

"Anything and everything he tells you to do. That's why Mr. McKay shows the old goats these movies—to give them ideas. We have connecting rooms, through the bathroom, and if you want me for anything, just rap on the door. Although I don't know what I can do for you, kid. You're in this, and you might as well make the best of it. If I sound hard, it's because I am hard, Maria. You aren't a baby, you're a big buxom woman, and you came into this business just like I did, for the money." Helen smiled wryly, and put her arm around Maria's shoulders. "Go on into your bedroom, Maria, and get undressed. You'll find a wrapper or robe of some kind to wear while you're waiting. Just look through the closet."

Dismissed, Maria went through the bathroom into Number Six, undressed and hung her clothing in the closet. She slipped into a loose, red cotton Japanese happi coat she found in the closet, and tied the belt in a loose bow at her waist. The bedroom was almost identical to the one she had waited in the night before, and as she smoked three cigarettes in a row, she looked distastefully at the square mirror above the bed and its matching mate on the wall.

When he entered the bedroom without bothering to knock, Maria's Mr. Smith was still laughing deep in his chest. His laughter changed abruptly into a racking paroxysm of coughing, his red face turned a brighter hue, and tears beaded the rims of his deep-set eyes. Under the bright fluorescent overhead lighting, Maria discovered that his eyes were a rich cobalt blue. Mr. Smith fumbled for a handkerchief during his coughing fit, opened the square of linen, and spat a gob of phlegm into the folds. Knitting his untrimmed shaggy white brows together, he examined the phlegm with intense concentration for several moments before folding and returning the handkerchief to his pocket.

"Did you see that Mexican cartoon, Maria?" he asked.

"No, sir. We girls aren't allowed to see the movies."

"You should see this one," he croaked humorously. "It's a scream!"

"Yes, sir. I'll ask Mr. McKay if I can see it some time."

Mr. Smith began to disrobe, handing each piece of clothing to Maria to hang in the closet for him as he removed it. Finally, Mr. Smith sat on the edge wearing his narrow, black patent leather slippers, black silk socks, and the tight black bands of garters gripping his white calves. Maria was both repelled and fascinated by the sight of his naked, flabby body. His flesh was a dead, slug-like white, and his meaty arms and legs were corded with twisted knots of blue veins. As Maria smiled tremulously, her eyes wide in disgusted fascination, Mr. Smith said: "Get me a glass of water from the bathroom, sweetie."

"Yes, sir," Maria whispered guiltily.

Mr. Smith removed a full set of gray dental plates from his mouth, placed them carefully on the bedside table, and Maria made a sudden swerve in direction and entered the hallway instead of the bathroom. Her feet carried her rapidly down the hallway, and she burst through the door of McKay's quiet study shouting.

"I won't go through with it, Mr. McKay! I'm through, do you hear me? Not with him or anybody else! I'm going home right now! Back to New York!" By this time McKay had left his desk and reached the girl. He slapped her face once with an open palm, grasped both of her shoulders firmly, and shoved her rudely into a chair. Maria gasped noisily, lapsed into dry-eyed, horror-stricken silence, and stared pleadingly at McKay.

"Control yourself, my dear," McKay said calmly. He opened a drawer in his desk, removed a legal-sized Manila folder, opened it, and handed an eight-by-ten inch glossy photograph to Maria. Automatically, Maria dropped her eyes from McKay's smiling face to the photograph in her hands.

"Rather a good likeness of you, isn't it?" McKay stated as he closed the Manila folder. "You may keep it if you like. I have several different poses of the same scene, and the negatives, and I can always make more for your friends. Tarzan wore a narrow black mask, as you can see. A wise precaution. Next time, perhaps you will do the same. Sanchez is a wonderful photographer. He's especially good with flowers. If you really want me to, Maria, I'll be glad to send a set of these photos to your mother in Manhattan, a set to Miss Peggy Vittorni, and another set to the personnel manager of the Faultless Topcoat Company."

"You wouldn't!" Maria cried out. "Nobody could do a thing like that!"

"Nobody?" McKay put the tips of his fingers together and smiled. "Are you sure, Maria? Really sure?"

Maria angrily tore the photo in half, put the halves together and ripped them across, tossed the pieces onto the floor.

"And now, my dear," McKay said, as he helped Maria out of the chair, "you have work to do. You shouldn't keep Mr. Smith waiting."

Without further argument, Maria walked slowly down the hall, paused a moment to square her shoulders, and opened the bedroom door.

"Where'd you go?" Mr. Smith said petulantly. "I told you to get me a glass of water!"

"In a minute, Mr. Smith." Maria smiled timidly in his general direction, keeping her eyes averted from his nude body, and crossed the bedroom to the bathroom. She rapped at the connecting door, called softly to Helen.

"What is it, Maria?" Helen said, opening the door a crack, a worried frown creasing her forehead.

"Let me have one of those yellow capsules, Helen. Two if you can spare them."

"Sure, honey, in a second." Helen closed the door, opened it a few moments later, and thrust a hand holding her jeweled pillbox through the narrow opening. Maria took the pillbox, and Helen quickly slammed her door. Maria swallowed two pills, drank a glass of water, refilled the glass and reentered her bedroom.

"Here's your water, Mr. Smith," she said lightly, placing the glass on the bedside table. "Do you mind if I switch out the overhead lights?"

"Yes, I do mind!" Mr. Smith replied crossly.

Maria forced her eyes to look at Mr. Smith. She spoke with weary resignation. "Anything you say, sir."

At six-thirty A.M. the following morning, Maria entered the lobby of the Rotunda Hotel, and crossed to the desk for her key. The night desk clerk, who didn't get relieved until eight A.M., smiled happily when she mentioned her room number.

"You sure have had the calls, Miss Dugan," he said brightly, handing her four slips of paper and her key. "All from New York. A Miss Vittorni once, at nine last night, and the other three from a Mr. Sidney Halper. His last call was at four A.M. He seemed pretty anxious to get in touch with you, Miss Dugan. Operator

Twenty-two, New York. If you want me to, I'll get the operator while you go upstairs, and you can take the call privately in your apartment.

Maria ripped the four slips of paper into several small pieces, held her hand straight out, level with her shoulder, and let the shreds of paper flutter to the carpet. The night clerk, a middle-aged man with a dozen years behind more than a dozen hotel desks, kept his smiling composure, revealed no surprise at the girl's imperious actions.

"Here are your instructions," Maria said coldly. "If there are any more long distance calls, you will tell the caller that I have checked out, leaving no forwarding address. You will pass these instructions on to the clerk who relieves you. These same instructions will be confirmed later today by the manager, Mr. Wallace, to all of you. Do you understand?"

"Yes, Miss Dugan," the night clerk said easily.

"Do you have any questions?"

"No, Miss Dugan. Your instructions will be carried out to the letter."

Maria opened her purse, placed a five-dollar bill on the blotter, and turned away toward the elevators. The clerk folded the bill into a small, tight square, stuffed it into his watch pocket.

"That sure is a cold one," he said beneath his breath. "As hard as nails."

SIXTEEN

A HARD loud slap across his right cheek woke Ralph from his late morning slumbers. As he scrambled to a sitting position, awakened rudely from his sound sleep, his feet became entangled in the sheet at the foot of the bed. His head was then rocked back against the headboard by another rough slap across the other side of his face.

Cursing with frustrated surprise and fury, Ralph groped for the sheet imprisoning his feet, got them disentangled, and lunged across the room.

Tarzan, after delivering his second blow, had retreated to the dresser, where he patiently watched Ralph's half-dazed fumbling with the sheet.

Cautiously, now that he recognized his attacker, Ralph advanced toward the bodyguard in a half-crouched position with tightened fists; fearfully, but with determination born of wrath. Tarzan leaned against the metal dresser, his long bare arms hanging loosely at his sides. Ralph feinted with a long cautious left, and attempted a right cross to the bodyguard's jaw. Tarzan took a swift left sidestep, blocked Ralph's amateurish blow by carelessly raising his left arm, dropped his chin to his chest, shuffled forward with a light skip, and buried his doubled right fist in Ralph's midriff. Driven backward by the force of the blow, Ralph fell heavily, reaching for the floor behind him to ease the shock of his fall. His head hit the metal bedrail as he fell, and as he struggled to regain another supply of air into his lungs, blood trickled from a jagged wound under his left ear.

Watching Ralph with alert, almost colorless blue eyes, Tarzan leaned against the dresser again and lighted a cigarette. The skillfully-planted blow in Ralph's solar plexus had removed his desire to fight. He recovered quickly, although his breathing was heavier than normal. He remained prudently where he had fallen, resting on his elbows, waiting for Tarzan to make the next move.

"You owe Mr. McKay three hundred dollars," Tarzan said flatly.

"I don't owe him anything!" Ralph said defiantly. He pulled himself up to a sitting position, looking warily at the bodyguard.

Breathing easier, he got to his feet, sat dizzily on the edge of the bed, fingered the swelling lump beneath his ear.

Tarzan picked up Ralph's wallet from the dresser, removed the money, and counted it. Smiling with his tongue between his teeth Tarzan said: "Where's the rest of it? There's only one hundred and seventy-six bucks here."

"I borrowed some money," Ralph replied. "And I had to repay it."

Tarzan returned two five-dollar bills to the wallet, folded the remaining bills, and shoved them into his trousers. He tossed the wallet at Ralph. It bounced off Ralph's bare chest and fell to the floor before he could get his hands on it.

"Mr. McKay said to leave you ten bucks for gas," Tarzan explained. "Get out of Miami Beach before sundown. That's an order."

"I don't take orders from you, or Mr. McKay either!" Ralph said bitterly. "I can live in Miami Beach or any place else! Who in the hell do you people think you are?"

"I'll check tonight to make sure you've left," Tarzan said quietly, ignoring Ralph's outburst.

"And what will you do if I haven't gone?" Ralph sneered. "Kill me? You people make me laugh!"

"No," Tarzan said quietly. "I won't kill you, Ralph. I'll break your legs." He dropped his cigarette to the floor and crushed it beneath his foot. "I'll tie you up and put you on the concrete floor of the garage out to the house. Then I'll drive back and forth across your legs with the Caddy."

For a long moment Ralph looked disgustedly at the bodyguard, and then his face paled beneath his tan. Tarzan's toneless announcement filled him with an unholy fear. By just looking at the bodyguard he could see that the man had no feelings or imagination. Tarzan would break his legs like the early American Indians had tortured their helpless captives, chopping off arms and legs to hear the funny noises the victims made, unable to put themselves in the other person's place...Ralph couldn't control the trembling of his hands and legs, but his voice was surprisingly firm.

"You go back to your boss and tell him I'm not running. Check back here tonight, next week, or next month, and I'll be sitting right here waiting for you!"

Tarzan shrugged indifferently, and left the room without closing the door. His feet, encased in a ragged pair of tennis shoes, were noiseless as he descended the stairs. Downstairs, the screen door slammed.

Ralph closed the bedroom door, leaned against it and listened to his excited heart beats, perspiration streaming down his face. Without bothering to dress first, Ralph got his suitcase from under the bed, opened it, and hastily began to pack his belongings.

There are worse things than being a coward, Ralph thought to himself as he tooled slowly along the highway towards Dania. He was driving at a slow twenty-five miles an hour. He made a lazy sweep with his left arm out the window to signal an impatient driver behind him that the way ahead was clear. He was running, yes, but he didn't have to race away from Miami Beach to Orlando like a frightened sheep!

And besides, there were several more hours before sundown.

Anybody would do the same, Ralph consoled himself. Was he any different from any other average American male?

Besides, Ralph knew he was yellow. He was proving it by running away from an ignorant, oversized brute with pale yellow hair who had promised to break his legs for him if he stayed. What else could he do? Why not be practical, for Christ's sake!

And Tommy Grant had agreed. After packing, Ralph had driven to the hotel to borrow one hundred dollars from Tommy, and explained the situation. Tommy had willingly advanced the money, told him that he was wise to leave, and had wanted to go with him. But Ralph had talked Tommy out of quitting.

"McKay has nothing against you, Tommy. Stick it out for the rest of the summer. You're saving money and if you went up to Orlando with me, Dad could only give us part time work anyway." They had shaken hands, Ralph had promised to mail Tommy a money order for the loan from Orlando, and he had driven away.

And now, Ralph thought bitterly, I am that most fortunate of men: The Live Coward! Mr. Average! The Corporation Slave-To-Be!

After being the direct cause of Maria's downfall, by failing her now, I also fail myself forever! I will never be the artist I wanted to be, following my own ideas, wrong or right; I'll end up in a sign shop some place, designing neon signs for the "Dew Drop Inn" motels and the "Bill's Place" bar-and-grills of Florida...

The gaudy motels along the ocean now had gaps between them as Ralph coasted along the highway. They were two- and three-hundred yards apart, and the expensive oceanfront lots in between, each with a bright FOR SALE — SEE YOUR BROKER sign, allowed Ralph to see the serene, blue-green ocean. Someday, Ralph thought, a person will drive down the East Coast from Jacksonville to Miami Beach without being able to see the Atlantic Ocean— unless he checks into a motel that has a private beach. Straight ahead, on his right, he saw what looked like a Spanish monastery, but an enormous neon sign announced in twisted, glowing tubes of blue that this was:

LOS PINOS MOTEL
SWIMMING POOL
PRIVATE BEACH
TELEVISION
SHUFFLE BOARDS
VACANCY

Ralph turned the wheel, braked in front of the office, and got out of his car. I'm not actually in Miami Beach, he justified his action; I'm halfway between Miami Beach and Dania. If I drive to Orlando now, staring this late in the day, I'll arrive about three in the morning, a hell of a time to get home. In the morning, maybe, I can get an early start.

If the exterior of the Los Piños Motel resembled a monastery, the resemblance stopped at the door to Ralph's room. His room was not a simple monk's "cell," by any means. Cost for a single: $12.00. Four walls, three in terracotta, one in dramatic black; red enameled doors; ultraviolet light warming the toilet seat, bathtub and shower; bathroom completely tiled. A television set with a twenty-four inch screen. Wall-to-wall carpets in thick golden nylon. Red brocade floor-to-ceiling drapes. An original nonobjective painting in a white frame centered on the black wall. Two sling chairs, one white, one tangerine. A low, three-quarter Hollywood bed; white clean-smelling sheets, covered by a Chinese red chenille bedspread. Three foam rubber pillows, each encased in white nylon pillowcases. A whispering air-conditioner mounted near the ceiling to allow an even circulation of cold air, keeping the guests out of a possible draught.

A middle-aged Negro, with a tonsure of gray hair around his shaven head, and wearing a red silk monk's habit, carried Ralph's suitcase into the room and placed it on the wrought-iron stand at the foot of the bed. He bowed low, made a swift exit, only to return a few moments later with a pitcher full of ice cubes, a bottle of soda, and a copy of the newspaper, all "compliments" of the management. Ralph tipped the "monk" a modest dollar for the "compliments," which was graciously accepted.

Ralph had requested and received a room as far off the highway as possible. His car could not be seen; more than thirty walls were between his carport and the highway. Using his mother's maiden name, he had registered as Ralph Jessup. He sat down in the tangerine chair. A good place to hide. He would have cheerfully accepted a lifetime sentence to this room, providing he never had to step outside.

"Everything could have been so different!" he said wistfully.

If he and Maria had gotten married, he could have quit school, borrowed some money from his father, and then built a small house for two on one of the small lakes near Orlando. They could have lived quietly, blissfully, in peace and solitude. They could have painted every morning, developing his style and technique, and then, after a concentrated four hours of work, Maria would call him to lunch. She would have been beautiful, her face flushed from the stove, a frilly white apron about her waist, and the food, of course, would have been heavenly. All of her love would be mixed into each course, like seasoning from Heaven. In the afternoon, they would fish and swim in their private lake, eat an early dinner, and get to bed before sundown for a full, exciting night of tender love-making...

Ralph rose to his feet and threw himself to the bed in an ecstasy of induced sentiment. But to his surprise, he was unable to cry. He was too practical. After two weeks at a lakeside retreat, City Girl Maria would have had him employed somewhere, complaining every night because there wasn't enough money coming in. She would have wanted an apartment in a city—Jacksonville, perhaps—clothes, jewelry, a new car; things, not him. And if he didn't hump to get them for her, she was the type to dump him for someone who would.

Maria would have made a lousy wife for me, Ralph thought, sitting up and lighting a cigarette. He loved her, yes, romantically and passionately, because of her youth, beauty, and musky animal magnetism, but he felt no real affection for her. How could he? He didn't even know her! But he did know himself fairly well after twenty-five years, and he wasn't going to run out on her without trying a second time. He could talk to her, anyway, beat some sense into her beautiful head with logic, get some facts of life into that thick skull!

Having made the decision, Ralph got through the rest of the afternoon and night without further worry or thought about what he would actually say to Maria. He sent out for dinner, watched television until midnight, and slept soundly until ten the next morning.

After his pleading twenty-minute telephone call, Maria reluctantly agreed to meet Ralph at the Los Piños Motel at noon. When she arrived in a taxi at twelve-fifteen, Ralph met her at the entrance and paid the driver. There was a self-confidence in Maria's manner that hadn't been there before, but Ralph attributed it to the new azure linen suit she was wearing, sensing an underlying feeling of insecurity in the girl. By putting himself in her place, he realized the enormous amount of will power it must have taken for Maria to visit him after the paces he had put her through in her apartment.

He made a few casual, offhand remarks about the weather, expressed admiration for her suit, and guided her to a reserved table beside the swimming pool. He ordered tropical fruit salads, iced tea, and smiled hesitantly, wetting his lips. Maria studied his apprehensive expression for a moment with frank earnest eyes, and then laughed.

"You remind me of a young boy trying to talk his mother into giving up cigarettes," she said with amusement.

"I haven't said anything yet," Ralph said, taken aback by the comparison.

Maria patted his hand. "I'm sorry, Ralph. I didn't mean that. Sitting out here in the sunlight, everything seems a little unreal to me. But I'm grown up now, Ralph. I feel old enough to be your mother, and you can't tell me anything I don't know already. So I'd rather you didn't try. Let's just sit here, enjoy our lunch, and pretend that nothing has happened."

"I can't." Ralph shook his head. "Do you know why I asked you to meet me here, away from Miami Beach?"

"It's very lovely here," Maria replied, looking about at the arcades and arches of the "monastery."

"No, it isn't," Ralph said hotly. "It's an architectural monstrosity, inaccurate in a thousand details. But I'm not here because I want to be. I was ordered to leave Miami by your friend, McKay. If I hadn't left, his bodyguard would have broken both my legs!"

"Yes?" Maria said without surprise.

"Doesn't that give you an idea of the kind of people you're mixed up with?"

"I know already." Maria shrugged. "And I'm adjusted to it."

"You can't be, Maria. No matter what McKay told you it was a lie. The more things he makes you do, the deeper you'll be involved. And then you'll never get out. This is the truth, Maria, God's truth!" Ralph ran fingers through his hair, searching for convincing words. "Right now, it still isn't too late. He doesn't know you're here, and if you just leave right now with me, I'll drive you all the way to New York. Once you're—"

"That's enough, Ralph," Maria said. "It was already too late when you asked me to leave before. I didn't know it then, but it was. Mr. McKay has photographs of me that he could send my family. I don't have to tell you the kind of photos they are. You have enough imagination to guess." Maria looked down at her plate. "So now you know. I couldn't leave if I wanted to, and after the things I've already gone through, I'm not so sure that I'd ever go, anyway…"

"Photographs can be bought, Maria! I don't know how much McKay has invested in you—I don't want to think about it—but suppose we offered to buy him off? I think I could get at least five thousand from my father. You could raise something, probably, from your family, and—"

"Five thousand is peanuts, Ralph. You mean well, but it's too late. Let's forget about it. This is all fresh fruit in this salad, isn't it?"

"Yeah. I guess so," Ralph said glumly.

For a few minutes both were silent. Unable to finish his salad, Ralph pushed the plate to one side and lit a cigarette. He looked thoughtfully at Maria.

"I'm not going to leave you, Maria," he said earnestly. "You don't have a single friend down here. No one. I feel rotten about this, because all of it's my fault."

"Don't blame yourself for my actions, Ralph. I don't."

"You're going to need me one day, and I'll be here. We can get together once in awhile. Tonight, maybe. Go to a movie. I don't know."

"I've got a date tonight. A man, a stranger, will call for me at eight. We'll go night-clubbing. I don't know who he is but he likes to have a pretty girl with him when he has a good time. When he gets through making the spots, we'll go back to my apartment and he'll spend the rest of the night with me in bed."

"You say that as if you didn't care!" Ralph exclaimed.

"I don't. I'll be paid well. Tomorrow night Mr. McKay is giving another party at his house in the 'Glades. Nine P.M. Again I'll be well paid. I'll sleep with an old man, maybe a famous man I never would have met otherwise. And I don't care, Ralph. Not anymore. If you think I'm cruel in telling you these things, I am. But I don't want you around. Go home, go back to college like a good boy. I like you, Ralph, but you can't afford a woman like me."

"Where is Mr. McKay now?"

"On the *Sea Witch*, I suppose. He isn't really such a bad person, Ralph. He spends all of the time he can out in the open. After so long, he's become so entangled in wickedness, he doesn't know any other way to live. That's what I think, anyway. Because I feel the same way."

"When do you girls go to his house?"

"Tomorrow night? About eight-thirty or nine. He and Tarzan get there about seven or seven-thirty. It's a dinner party tomorrow as well, a catered affair. So I suppose they'll be there fairly early to arrange things. Why?"

"I just wondered," Ralph said abstractedly.

"Thanks for the lunch, Ralph." Maria stood up, brushed imaginary crumbs from her skirt. "I see my cab is back. I told him to return in half an hour."

"I wasted my time, didn't I?" Ralph said, as they walked beneath the arcade to the waiting taxi in front of the office.

"No," Maria smiled. "It was a much more pleasant way to say goodbye. Not like the last time." She reached out a gloved hand. They shook hands formally, and Ralph closed the door when Maria climbed into the back seat. Holding her elbow close to her side, Maria waggled her fingers, smiled again, and the cab made the long U-turn down the middle of the court. When the cab passed him again, picking up speed toward the exit, Ralph followed it a few yards in the driveway and shouted:

"Goodbye, Maria!"

Ralph returned to his room, sat down in the tangerine chair, and studied his curling fingers. In a matter of days, hours really, McKay and Tarzan had transformed a young and beautiful girl into a cold and callous woman. She was as hard as a brand-new ten-ply tire! He felt absolutely nothing for her now. Not pity, or sympathy, or tenderness, or love, or desire. Nothing. Nothing!

Because he felt nothing, he was going to kill McKay and Tarzan. Wipe them off the face of the earth. How? Ralph moved his chair to the desk, and with a ballpoint pen and a piece of motel stationery, began to list the things he would need...

SEVENTEEN

PERHAPS Ralph was a little mad. If so, and he suspected that he was, he was a methodical madman. He worked and re-worked his plans and requirements with the thoroughness of a Prussian lieutenant preparing his first field exercise. He accepted the initial idea that popped into his mind; the idea was sound, and he stuck to it doggedly, listing possible flaws, meeting each objection with a counter-attack.

Ten hours of sleep before meeting Maria had something to do with the keenness of his mind, but the very real knowledge of the danger represented by Tarzan's promise had also sharpened his thinking. He moved about his work with boldness tempered by cunning.

By six that evening, Ralph was seated at a corner table in the Munchen Beer Garden. Draught beer, two bits per glass, a pitcher for a dollar. A half-filled pitcher sat before him on the red and white masonite table, and Ralph sipped his beer slowly, restlessly watching the three exits in the latticed walls. The three exits were three reasons why Ralph had chosen the alfresco beer garden as the place to meet Johnny Townsend. Tarzan could hardly enter all three doors at the same time; he could only come in by one of them, which left two for Ralph to get away. Why shouldn't he play everything as safely as possible?

If he was going to be a murderer, and that was his decision, two broken legs would not be an asset to his plans. It's them or me, Ralph thought grimly, and it isn't going to be me!

Townsend had been pleased by the telephone call, and Ralph was positive the boy would show up on time. But whether he did or not, the night would be a long one, and if he had to he could get along without Johnny's assistance. To make his senses more alert than ever, Ralph decided that one more dexedrine tablet wouldn't do him any harm. He swallowed a pill, and chased it down with beer. No more, he mused; that makes three since noon.

Johnny Townsend entered the 91st Street entrance, purchased four quarter beer coupons from the cashier, and sauntered across the room jauntily, pulled out a chair and sat down.

"You didn't have to get coupons, Johnny," Ralph said. "I've got a pitcher already, and an extra glass."

"Fine," Johnny grinned. "You drink your pitcher and I'll drink mine." He stopped a passing waiter and ordered a pitcher of beer. "While I wait, I'll have a glass out of yours." Johnny filled his glass, drained it, and puffed out his lips noisily. The ring of foam on his upper lip made a comic moustache.

"How're things at the Rotunda?" Ralph said easily.

"Like always. Found another job yet?"

"Haven't looked."

"You'll find something. Anything would be better than that night elevator. If I could only get a few bucks ahead I'd quit myself. I haven't paid my room rent in two weeks now, but as long as I have a job the old witch knows I'm good for it and won't throw me out. But if I quit, bang!" Johnny laughed with genuine amusement. "She'd toss me out in a minute and keep all three pairs of my jeans for security!"

Ralph narrowed his eyes. "Johnny, I lied to you on the phone. I don't have two dames lined up for tonight."

"That's okay, Ralph. Women are not a problem. There's plenty. Money is the problem. When I pick up a girl I have my principles, and I don't feel right unless I buy at least one drink!"

He's a surprisingly good-natured kid, Ralph thought. But as long as I don't tell him anything, he can't get into trouble. Ralph took a tightly-folded twenty-dollar bill out of his shirt pocket, unfolded it, smoothed out the wrinkles, and slipped it under the edge of Johnny's newly-delivered pitcher of beer.

"Don't think I was hinting around for a loan, Ralph," Johnny said anxiously. "Especially when you're out of a job!"

"That isn't a loan, Johnny. I want you to do something for me, and the twenty is yours. No loan. A payment for service."

"Do you want me to beat somebody up, Ralph?" Johnny grinned and flexed his biceps.

"No," Ralph said sternly. "But it's a serious proposition. And it could be dangerous. I'll explain, and if you don't want to do it, there are no hard feelings, and you can keep the twenty anyway. Just for keeping your mouth shut. Don't tell anybody you saw me, no matter what happens, not even my buddy, Tom Grant."

"I know how to keep my mouth shut, Ralph. I may kid around

a lot and everything, but on something serious, well—"

"I trust you, Johnny. That's why I called you." Ralph refilled his glass. "Go ahead. Put the twenty in your wallet."

Johnny did as he was told. "Now I can pay my room rent, but I won't." He sighed. "Well, what is it, Ralph? I'll do it."

"Don't agree just yet. As far as you're concerned, this is a gag. Got that? A gag."

"Sure."

"At one A.M. tonight, go into the employees' locker room at the Rotunda and change into your uniform. Nobody'll be in there then. Now. You're changed. Go out the back door, beat it across the parking lot to the gate of the new building site. By the way, do you know the night watchman over there, where the new hotel is going up?"

"No, I don't even know what he looks like."

"That isn't important. I've seen him plenty of times on my breaks. He stands at the gate and smokes most of the time, watching the traffic on the highway. That is, when he isn't watching the women undress in the hotel. He's in plain view of the guests on the north side of the hotel. About once an hour he makes a tour inside the fence, and then stands by the gate again. This isn't going to be easy, Johnny."

"Just tell me what you want me to do," Johnny said impatiently.

"This guy's in his early forties, fifty at the most, and I think he'll go for this. Tell him there's a rich woman on the sixth floor who has been admiring him every night from her window and wants to meet him. Say that she sent you out to bring him up to her room for a drink. Flash the twenty. Tell the old boy she gave it to you to get him up there. After he agrees to go with you—"

"Suppose he don't? What woman on Six is this, anyway?"

"There isn't any such woman, Johnny. You just tell him there is. And I think he'll go with you. I'm paying you twenty bucks; it's up to you to convince him how beautiful this imaginary woman is. Lie like hell, the way you do to Old Sourball, the bell captain." Ralph smiled, lit a cigarette.

Johnny laughed. "Okay, I'll talk him into going with me. Then what? If he's afraid to leave his post, I could tell him that he can watch the gate from the woman's room. Right?"

"That's the idea. Go through the locker room, take the service elevator and somehow, get it jammed between the fourth and fifth floor. You know how to jam it, don't you?"

"Easy. All you have to do is unscrew that little nut—"

"How you do it isn't important, Johnny, but do it. And keep it stuck for at least an hour. From approximately one-fifteen to two-fifteen."

"Suppose the super or room waiters want to use it?"

"They can't, because it's stuck."

"Yeah, I suppose. There's no food service after midnight anyway."

"That's right. The superintendent is the only man you'd have to worry about, and it's unlikely that he'd use the elevator after midnight."

"That could be a damned unpleasant hour in there with that night watchman!" Johnny laughed.

"Twenty bucks an hour," Ralph reminded.

"Yeah. Sure. But then what? Unseen, I work on the handle, slip the screw back in, and the elevator's working again. What do I do with the night watchman when I get to the sixth floor?"

"There isn't any woman, so take him down again. The way I have it figured, Johnny, after an hour, he'll be anxious to get back to his job to see if there's a steam shovel or something missing. Don't you agree?"

"I agree." Johnny drank two swift glasses of beer in succession, looked unsmilingly at Ralph. "Will there be a steam shovel missing?"

"No. If you don't know anything, you can't tell anything. But you won't have to. There may be a few things missing from the site, but do you honestly believe the night watchman would tell his bosses that the items were taken while he was stuck between the fourth and fifth floor of the Rotunda? He'd be a damned fool. If he's smart, he'll put on the dumb act."

"Suppose he doesn't? At the very least, I'll be out of a job—if I'm not in jail!"

"No, you won't. This little gag should go off without a hitch. But suppose it doesn't? If nobody sees you, you can say the watchman is a liar. If you are seen, caught getting out of the elevator, and the watchman spills about you, clam up till you talk to Mr.

Wallace. Tell the manager that there was such a woman, and that she did give you a twenty to pick up the watchman for her. Give him a guest's name. He'll believe you. But tell him you'll never spill it to the police, because it would reflect on the hotel. Wallace'll get you out of it, and you might even end up with a better job because of your 'great loyalty.'"

Johnny was silent. With a finger, he wrote his name in suds on the top of the damp table.

"What's the matter, John? Aren't there any women on the sixth floor?"

"At least a dozen, Ralph. I'll go through with it, even though I don't know what the score is. I can use the twenty. But I'm worried about you. Are you in some kind of trouble, Ralph? I mean, to steal something—that isn't right. You don't have to do that. If you need money, I'll bet you could get five or six hundred out of that custom Ford of yours."

"It's only a gag, Johnny. Nothing else. But no matter what happens, you haven't seen me since I quit. All I need is an hour. From one-fifteen till two-fifteen. After you take the watchman down to the basement, change your clothes, and you're through."

Johnny pushed his pitcher toward Ralph. "You drink the rest of it, Ralph. I don't want anymore. But you'll get your hour tonight. You can count on it."

"Thanks." The two men shook hands. Johnny left by the 91st Street exit, and Ralph faded out through the rear door to Datura Street where had had parked his car. Ralph climbed into his car and drove out Highway One to a drive-in movie, getting there in plenty of time to catch the first showing at seven-fifteen.

Ralph coasted past the blazing lights of the Rotunda Hotel entrance, slowed down as he passed the service entrance, and cut his lights. He pulled off the highway one hundred yards past the gate of the new building site, on the grass, and stopped behind a giant-sized bulldozer. There were two red lanterns in front of the yellow bulldozer, and two more behind, although the machine was parked well off the highway. He looked at his wristwatch: 1:20 A.M. With luck, he had fifty-five minutes. Plenty of time.

Ralph cut the engine, slid across the seat, and got out of his car on the right side, a tire iron on his hand. Hugging the fence, staying well within its deep shadows, he inched his way soundlessly toward the gate. If Johnny had done his job, the watchman wouldn't be at his post. If the watchman was at the gate, Ralph planned to crush his skull with the tire iron.

The watchman was gone. The gate was closed, but unlocked. A loop of heavy chain held the slatted, wooden doors closed, but luckily the large padlock between the links had been left unlocked. A moment later, Ralph was inside the enclosure, walking surefootedly toward the red wooden shack marked EXPLOSIVES, playing a pencil flashlight on the broken ground to light his way. There were two hasps on the wooden door of the shack, each securely fastened by a padlock, but the tire iron ripped them off easily.

Ralph made three trips from the explosives shack to his car. His first two trips were made cautiously, the first with an unopened box of dynamite, the second with three loops of primacord around his neck, a box of detonating caps held gingerly in each hand. His final trip was made hurriedly, after dumping two reels of heavy wire, a battery blaster, a pair of crimping pliers, and a dozen spools of copper wire into a burlap sack he found in the shack. Before leaving the red shack, Ralph closed the door, but didn't attempt to pound the hasps back into place. If the watchman discovered the break-in within the hour, or before morning, that was his problem. Ralph had what he came after.

An hour later Ralph was back in his room at the Los Piños Motel. He dropped the venetian blinds over the wide, single window to the court, pulled the brocaded drapes closed, and brought all of his pilfered items on his carefully prepared list. He was still short two rolls of adhesive tape, but he could pick them up at a drugstore on his way to McKay's house tomorrow afternoon. The battery inside the blaster was an old one, so he decided to buy a new one at a hardware store when he purchased the tape. Otherwise, he was all set. Everything checked except his manual dexterity.

Ralph had gone through the six-week course in demolitions at Fort Benning, and he knew something about explosives, but how much did he remember? The vibration of the detonating caps for dynamite had to be the same frequency as the dynamite. According to the information on the box, that checked. And he had also taken another box of caps to match the primacord. He flexed his fingers, held them out beneath the light on the desk and studied them. A slight tremor in the tips. Not from nervousness, but caused by the dexedrine, he reflected.

Cutting two short lengths of copper wire, Ralph experimented by wiring the ends to a detonating cap. Even with the slight tremor in his fingers, he could manage all right. He removed the wires from the cap carefully as he had attached them, repacked the caps in the cardboard box.

He reloaded the turtleback of his car with the explosives, dropped the lid gently, snapped the chair lock on his door, and undressed for bed. He would have preferred to keep the explosives in the room, but he remembered in time that fumes from a box of dynamite had been known to give a person in headache.

Ralph snapped out the lights, smoked a contemplative cigarette in the dark while sitting naked on the edge of his bed, snuffed out the butt in the ashtray and fell asleep within twenty minutes.

EIGHTEEN

RALPH Tone's disguise was simple but effective. When he purchased the battery for his stolen blaster in the hardware store, he also bought a gallon can of unneeded white lead paint. By buying paint, he had been given free, a white cheesecloth painter's cap with a black cardboard bill. He wore the cap on his head, the bill pulled well down over his eyes.

When he bought the rolls of medical adhesive tape in the drugstore he also purchased a sack of tobacco. The round yellow tag swung outside the single pocket on the breast of his dark blue T-shirt. A useless purchase, he thought, but a lot of workmen roll their own, and little touches add authenticity. He was wearing a faded pair of blue jeans, and brown oxfords without socks. The shoes were fairly new, but he had scuffed the toes on the concrete floor of the carport before checking out of the Los Piños Motel at noon. Three fingers rubbed across the lower edge of his car engine, and then brushed lightly against his right check completed his disguise.

Precisely at four P.M., Ralph turned boldly into the Everglades Estates, glancing up distastefully at the faded letters on the arch. The afternoon sun reflected from the fresh yellow gravel. To prevent possible skidding in the thick road covering, he slowed his speed to twenty miles per hour. If there was more than one car parked in front of McKay's house, Ralph planned to circle through the driveway with a swift turn and leave the area as quickly as possible. But there was just one car. The only car in sight was an old Plymouth, which probably belonged to the houseboy.

Ralph braked three feet beyond the doorway, picked his toolbox up from the front seat, and concealed a tire iron in his left hand by holding his arm close to his side. He climbed the steps, pushed the buzzer, and while he waited, kept his oil-streaked cheek toward the door, holding his tool box in his right hand.

The door opened to the length of the inside chain lock, and the houseboy's brown face peeped through the crack.

"Repairman," Ralph announced gruffly. "Mr. McKay called me out."

"There's nothing wrong here," Sanchez said.

"Look, buddy, I don't give a damn!" Ralph said, jiggling his toolbox noisily. "If you don't want the stove modified, okay, but I'm not making another trip out here!"

The door closed, the chain was unfastened, and the door swung open. Ralph tossed his toolbox through the open door, changed the tire iron to his right hand, and brought it down hard between Sanchez' neck and shoulder as he stepped inside the door. Knocked off balance, the houseboy screamed with pain in a high frightened voice, turned and ran. Ralph chopped viciously at the back of the houseboy's head, and succeeded in knocking the smaller man to the floor. Still conscious, Sanchez huddled on the floor, held both hands on top of his bleeding head, and whimpered:

"Please, please, please, please, please! Please, please please!"

Ralph opened his toolbox, removed precut lengths of copper wire prepared for the purpose, and wired the houseboy's feet together. Sanchez put up no resistance, and submitted to the cruel binding of his feet and the wiring of his hands behind his back without struggling. Ralph closed and locked the door, then turned the houseboy over on his back.

"Where are the photos?" Ralph asked.

"Photos?" Sanchez said, staring wild-eyed at Ralph.

Ralph kicked the smaller man in the ribs. "Photos."

"In the safe," Sanchez whispered.

"Where's the safe?"

"Behind the painting." Sanchez turned his frightened face toward the wall, tried to point out the Kandinsky with his popping eyes.

Ralph crossed to the painting, swung it open, and examined the safe. He picked up the tire iron again, advanced on the helpless houseboy. "Do you know the combination?" he said, raising the heavy iron above his head.

"No, sir!" Sanchez squealed. "I do not know! Please, please, please!" He began to cry. Ralph studied the wet brown face on the floor with narrowed eyes and decided that the man was telling the truth. Ralph opened the front door, removed his equipment, placed the box of dynamite behind a sparkleberry bush, and brought his rolls of wire, caps, and other purchases inside. He got into his car again circled around the driveway, and backed into the piney woods across the gravel road. He had to back and file several times to conceal his car behind the trees.

Ralph returned to the house and went to work.

Ralph looked at his watch. Seven P.M. The sun was down, and the remaining light in the sky was a pale nacreous gray. A few ragged wisps of orange clouds in the west scudded above the crooked black outline of the swamp. Within a few minutes it will be all over, Ralph thought. Any moment now, McKay and Tarzan will arrive; and when the door buzzer is pressed, they will be killed. Would he really solve anything by deliberately murdering them?

No. Others will take their place. As long as there are men and women in the world there will be sex. All kinds of sex. When men have money, lots of money, they will experiment, drive their jaded desires to fresh experimentation. And there will always be men like McKay to provide new thrills, fresh young girls, different entertainment. And there will always be more girls like Maria; willing recruits, attracted by fabulous sums of money...

But Maria, at least, will be free. In all likelihood, he was too late. She had had a taste of the money, excitement, and it was highly probable that she would stay on in Miami Beach, picking up men and selling herself to the highest bidder. A beautiful girl can always make money with her body, even when her contacts are destroyed.

At least I'll have given her this chance to break free, Ralph thought selflessly, and killing McKay will do it. There isn't any other way!

There was a sound of gravel banging into metal down the road. Ralph looked up from the wheel. His heart thumped wildly inside his chest. A car pulled into the driveway in front of McKay's house, a long yellow Cadillac convertible. Two men got out of the front seat, one on each side. The rear door opened and there was a flash of white dress in the dusk, topped by a crown of black hair.

"Maria!" Ralph screamed, but he didn't make a sound. The girl's name had only echoed inside his brain.

There was an explosion, a muffled boom that silenced the forest insects. Ralph got out of his car, pounded across the road, across the broad expanse of lawn. Chunks of concrete, plaster, and jagged splinters of hard wood covered the porch and the rug inside the doorway.

"These aren't dead people," Ralph said quietly. "They can't be. This one is a Gila monster, that one is an alligator. The brown one inside the door is a toad, and she—she's a black widow spider."

Ralph turned away and staggered across the lawn. His arms hung limply at his sides. They didn't swing with the motion of his body. His brown eyes were dull, fixed on nothing. He didn't remember opening the door of his car and sliding under the wheel...

Six weeks later Ralph Tone had a visitor. Except for another patient at the far end playing cards by himself, Ralph was the only man in the ward. It was mid-afternoon and the other forty-eight patients were scattered in various workshops throughout the hospital for occupational therapy. He sat quietly in a gray metal folding chair by the foot of his bed, looking down at the shiny, brown linoleum floor, silently moving his lips.

The wire-mesh door was unlocked at the war entrance, but Ralph didn't look up when the two men entered. One of them was a doctor, wearing a white, stiffly-starched, three-quarter length coat. The other man wore a conservative, gray business suit, and carried a narrow-brimmed straw hat in his right hand. The two men stopped in front of Ralph, and the doctor lifted Ralph's chin with his right hand.

"You've got a visitor, Ralph," the doctor said kindly. "This is Mr. Sidney Halper. He flew down from New York to ask you some questions about Maria Dugan."

Ralph turned his eyes uncomprehendingly on Sidney Halper's white face. The visitor's high forehead was shiny from recent contact with the sun, and he wore a pair of silver-rimmed glasses over a prominent nose.

"Anything at all you can tell me about Maria will be appreciated," Sidney began earnestly. "If we only knew your reasons, something—if I could take some kind of information back to Maria's mother..."

Ralph lowered his head.

"I screamed 'Maria!' as loud as I could," he said tonelessly. "There was an explosion, a muffled boom that silenced the forest insects. I got out of my car and ran across the road, across the lawn. Chunks of concrete, plaster, and jagged splinters of hard wood covered the porch and the rug inside the doorway." Ralph shook his head from side to side sorrowfully.

"These aren't dead people," Ralph pointed to the floor with stiff fingers. "They can't be. This one is a Gila monster, that one is an alligator. The brown one inside the door is a toad, and she—she's a black widow spider."

The doctor closed Ralph's mouth gently with an open palm, held it closed for a moment before he dropped his arm. Ralph silently moved his lips, looked intently at the floor.

Sidney Halper wiped his forehead with a handkerchief. The doctor took his arm and they turned away, moved toward the locked door. The doctor accompanied Sidney Halper through the corridors to the waiting room, stepped outside on the porch with him for a cigarette while the visitor waited for his taxicab to come up from the parking lot.

"That's it, Mr. Halper," the doctor said. "Just like a needle stuck in a record. The same thing over and over."

"But for how long?" Sidney asked, putting on his hat. "If it's only a matter of days, I could probably stay down a little longer."

"It may be five minutes, and it may be five years." The doctor shrugged. "Maybe never. One thing, he'll never be tried, even if he does come out of it. A trial would undoubtedly shock him right back into it. That would be my recommendation, anyway."

"It's terrible!" Sidney Halper shuddered in the hot sunlight. "To just *sit* there, seeing the same thing over and over…"

The doctor laughed, tossed his cigarette into the driveway. "Oh I don't know, Mr. Halper. Ralph hasn't got it so bad. He's gained ten pounds already. He's on tranquilizers. We're going to try electroshock therapy when we get around to it. He sleeps well every night, eats well. If you want to feel sorry for somebody, feel sorry for me. I've got seventy-three patients. Last night I only had three hours sleep!"

"I suppose you're right at that, Doctor." They shook hands. "I've got to get back to work myself. This wasted trip cost me four days off the job."

I wouldn't call a trip to Florida wasted. Didn't you do anything down here at all?"

Sidney laughed, winked behind his glasses. "Yes, I was lucky. I picked up a damned nice-looking blonde last night at the Miramar Bar. So I did get *something* taken care of."

The cab pulled up and Sidney descended the steps, opened the door, and waved. "Thanks for everything, Doctor. Thanks a lot. I know how busy you are."

"I didn't do anything. Nice meeting you, Mr. Halper."

The cab drove away. The doctor waved a friendly goodbye and hurried back inside the hospital. "Only a few minutes in the sun," he thought, "and I'm sweating like hell. Thank God the hospital has air-conditioning."

THE END